REBEL

A TIBETAN ODYSSEY

▾ ▾ ▾

CHERYL AYLWARD WHITESEL

HarperCollins*Publishers*

Library of Congress Cataloging-in-Publication Data
Whitesel, Cheryl Aylward.
Rebel: a Tibetan odyssey / Cheryl Aylward Whitesel.
p. cm.
Summary: Although he rebels against life in the Tibetan Buddhist monastery
where he had been sent, fourteen-year-old Thunder comes to some amazing
realizations about himself.
ISBN 0-688-16735-7
1. Tibet (China)—Juvenile fiction. [1. Tibet (China)—Fiction. 2. Buddhism—
Fiction. 3. Monks—Fiction.] I. Title. PZ7.W58785 Re 2000 [Fic]—dc21
99-45556

10   9   8   7   6   5   4   3   2   1
❖
First Edition

FOR MY PARENTS,

WARREN AND PATRICIA AYLWARD WHITESEL,

WITH LOVE AND THANKS

WHEN THE IRON BIRD FLIES AND HORSES MOVE ON WHEELS,

TIBETANS WILL BE SCATTERED LIKE ANTS AROUND THE WORLD,

AND THE TEACHINGS OF LORD BUDDHA

WILL COME TO THE LAND OF THE RED MAN.

—PROPHECY OF PADMASAMBHAVA, EIGHTH CENTURY

➤*A glossary may be found on pages 188–190.*

R·E·B·E·L

1

▾ ▾ ▾

THUNDER STOOD WHERE the ground slanted up and the wind whipped his hair. Below him a caravan of traders and yaks snaked through the narrow pass that led into this valley from the world beyond. His uncle and his brother Joker struggled down the sheer path toward their village. But Thunder hung back, spellbound by the shaggy yaks lumbering along under the ash-colored sky, the bells strung around their necks tinkling now and then. It fascinated him that strangers found their way here only to leave at once and roam far away.

Like all Tibetan caravans, this one was made up of people and animals, but no carts. An ancient prophecy said that when wheeled vehicles came to Tibet, the country would be conquered by foreigners—*fringies.*

"Let's go see the traders!" Thunder called to the others. He wanted to bury his nose in the yaks' tangled fur and find out once and for all whether, coming from so far away, they smelled different from the village yaks.

But as he started down the shale toward the caravan, Second Uncle Tendruk shouted back at him, "Thunder, no closer! They're fringies."

Reluctantly Thunder turned away from the caravan and followed his uncle. "Fringies, Second Aku Tendruk?" he asked. "No, they're Tibetan yaks and Tibetan traders."

"They're not from our village," Tendruk growled. "That's fringie enough." With a tight jaw Tendruk nodded at the can of wildflowers at Thunder's feet. They had spent the afternoon in the meadow above their village of Chu Lungba, collecting herbs to pound into medicine. Now they were on their way home.

Thunder picked up the can. But walking backward to catch a last glimpse of the caravan, he soon lagged behind again. From a distance he spun around and burst out, "Second Aku, why do you always hold me back from talking to the traders?"

"Talking to traders is not our way!" Tendruk barked, his eyes furious as he looked back at Thunder.

But Thunder raised his voice, running over his uncle's words in a rush: "You say fringie, but what do *you* know about fringies? Have you ever been outside Tibet? Or even outside our valley?"

"Brazen questions!" Tendruk shouted, striding toward Thunder with his fist up.

Thunder stuck out his chin and opened his mouth to argue, then realized that Tendruk looked ready to hit him. He bowed his head instead.

They went on hiking in silence for several minutes before Tendruk added in a tight voice, "I know only one thing about fringies, but Thunder, one thing is enough. Any fringie in Tibet must be killed."

"Because they are like evil spirits," Joker added.

"No more talk about such things," Tendruk commanded.

Their feet crunched rhythmically on the gravel. "Did you know the world is enormous, Aku?" Thunder asked timidly. "It holds five other countries besides Tibet."

Tendruk was gripping the handle of his can hard. "That's not true."

"It *is* true!" Thunder insisted. "The peddler told me himself, and you know he travels everywhere. He even told me the countries' names. They are China, Queenvictoria, California, England, and Minestrone. Aku . . ." Thunder looked across at Tendruk. What was the use of keeping secrets that would come out sooner or later? "Aku, I want to be a trader myself someday," he said in a rush. "I want to see—"

"We're not traders, I tell you! That's not our way! Now silence! Who knows which evil spirits are listening?" This time Tendruk strode away, leaving his nephews behind.

"Aku," Thunder called weakly, but Tendruk only dashed his hand through the air as he stalked off.

Joker stomped after Tendruk, imitating his walk. But after a few yards he spun around, laughing, and skipped back to Thunder.

"Stop it," Thunder muttered, but when Joker's expression turned worried, Thunder cuffed him good-naturedly. "Silly Bones," he said with a chuckle. "Look who thinks he knows about serious things like evil spirits and fringies."

"Of course I know about evil spirits," Joker chirped. "Children sense their presence. And you heard Second Aku, fringies are practically evil spirits, too. Or worse. You are as naughty to talk about one as about the other."

"I didn't say even one naughty thing about evil spirits," Thunder said, but he closed his hand over the silver charm box he always wore on a yak-hair cord around his neck to protect himself from demons.

"You talked about fringies, and that's not our way!" Joker cried as he scampered up the path in front of his brother.

"I did not."

"I'm scaring you! I *am*!"

"You are not! Besides, if *you* can sense evil spirits, so can I."

"No, no, no," Joker said, shaking his head. "Fourteen is too old. Look up there, the evil spirits are coming for you already. The sky is gray because they're wearing gray *chubas*!"

"They're coming for *you*. Now stop it!" Thunder commanded. "It isn't funny!" His can knocked against Joker's leg, spilling most of the flowers onto the path.

But Joker never knew when to quit. "It is *so* funny," he said. "Evil spirits are coming after you, but they can't catch me!" He shot over the crest of the hill and was gone.

"Joker! Get back here!" Thunder stared after him, waiting for him to come skipping back like before. When he didn't, Thunder looked toward where the traders had been. But they had disappeared, too. He sighed and began to gather the spilled flowers, expecting Joker to appear any minute and wrestle him to the ground.

He straightened up and looked around, realizing with a jolt that a storm was looming all around him. Rain clouds were rolling in overhead; the juniper bushes flapped hard.

Soon it was raining, and before he could collect all the flowers, those on the ground were transparent and limp.

The yaks and traders were gone; Second Aku was gone; Joker was gone. The flooded path was a dirty blur as he set off, his boots heavy with mud, his chuba sticking to his body like paint. "Joker!" he called, his hands cupped around his mouth. "Come back here, Joker! It's dangerous!"

Soon the sky was an eerie and violent black. The wind rushed like low-whistling breath into a bottle; the bushes shuddered. When a lightning bolt tore up the sky, he saw a string of prayer flags, suspended between two trees, snap off and flash away like a flying serpent. "Joker!" he shrieked again, but the wind was too loud; he could hardly hear his own voice.

His feet slipped out from under him as he made his way up and down muddy hillsides. He dropped his flower can and watched it clatter down the steep embankment, spilling water and his last ruined flowers into the mud.

By the time he'd slogged as far as the next pasture, he was staggering under the weight of his wet chuba, as heavy as rocks. He slopped into the dark water, but his boots sank deep into the muck. He stood fixed there, peering down at a murky shape sticking up out of the floodwater. When lightning flashed again, he could see that the shape was a drowned lamb, swaying with its eye opened skyward in death.

Like a punch in the face, it hit Thunder that he wasn't going to find his brother. "Joker," he moaned, covering his face with his hands. Then he staggered back to the flooded field's rim, found a sheltered spot under a rock ledge, and squatted there, shivering. The water poured over the ledge above him like a waterfall.

2

▼   ▼   ▼

THUNDER WOKE TO find himself on a felt blanket in a grassy glade with a Hair of Buddha tree, a willow, swaying overhead. A sheepskin lay heaped on his feet, and a chuba was folded under his head to form a pillow. As he lifted himself onto his elbows, the sun flashed through the branches above.

Thunder looked around. Nearby a young man stood tightening the saddle pack on a mule. Farther away through the trees several men were squatting around a tent, one crumbling the corner of a tea brick into a tea can. As Thunder stirred, the man near the mule turned to look at him. "Awake?" he asked.

"Where am I? Who are you?" Thunder asked. His voice came out squawky, and his throat was sore; swallowing hurt even more. He fell back, closing his eyes again. He felt so achy that even sitting up hurt.

"Open up!"

It was a moment before Thunder opened his eyes again. When he did, he found the man kneeling right at his side. He smelled exotic and unfamiliar. His chuba brushed against Thunder's chest. He pushed a little bottle of pink liquid against Thunder's teeth. Startled, Thunder jerked away. He'd never seen such a tiny bottle, and he didn't like that the man knelt so close.

"Drink it," the man commanded.

The man's accent was just peculiar enough to unsettle Thunder, and almost against his own will he complied. As the liquid rolled down the back of his throat, the soreness turned to numb warmth. Thunder fell back in surprise. He'd heard that certain foods or drinks were magical but had never experienced such a mystical process himself.

"Help?"

Thunder blinked in amazement, then nodded and put out his tongue to show his respect. He winced as he forced out the words: "Are you a sorcerer?"

The man gave him an odd glance but didn't answer.

"More," Thunder said, gesturing toward the bottle.

But the man shook his head. "Too much is no good. Go home."

"But where am I? And who are you?"

The stranger's eyes darted left and right. "I found you after the storm. You're lucky you lived through it."

There was something odd about the man, but Thunder couldn't put his finger on what it was—perhaps the horsey shape of his face or his big feet. "Who are you?" he asked. "You're so—"

"Go home! Go home!" the man urged, making shooing gestures.

Instead Thunder sank back and closed his eyes. Images floated into his mind, then vanished like smoke. A picture formed of Second Aku's angry face as he strode away. Yaks in the distance; wet flowers all over the ground. Then Thunder saw himself scrabbling in the mud; he remembered the sting of rain. A strand of prayer flags whipping around like a kite when the lightning flashed. Later, the dead eye of a lamb.

Joker.

"Did you find another boy?" he shrilled, hoisting himself up again. "Seven years old?"

"No."

A hundred fears leaped into his mind. He groaned and tottered to his feet. Choking on the pain in his throat, he reeled and fell against the trunk of the Hair of Buddha tree. "How long have I been here?" he croaked.

"Two days."

"I'd been talking about . . . evil spirits," Thunder managed to explain between painful swallows. "I said some things . . . I angered the demons. If—if they've taken my brother . . ." He squeezed his eyes shut.

"Hallucinations," the man muttered.

"What?"

The man glanced up sharply, then looked away.

"But I talked openly about . . . well, don't you see what I mean?" Thunder pondered how such horror—storm, sickness, kidnapping—could all be brought on by a few words spoken about fringies. He shook his head slightly to clear it. "I must go home now," he said, "and see if my brother . . . but yes, he *will* be there. And then I'll eat a prayer written on rice paper, and that'll cure this sickness."

"Eat a prayer," the man scoffed under his breath.

The man's odd odor, his peculiarly shaped face, these bizarre comments . . . Thunder peered at him, feeling wary. "But my *aku* blessed it," he said. Then, as if he'd been slapped, he understood. Backing away, he breathed, "You're a fringie."

The stranger's body twitched with shock. He stared at Thunder with a lot of white showing in his eyes and his nostrils flared. He said in a deadly tone, "I saved your life."

Thunder felt as if he'd been knocked flat. He put both hands to his temples.

"If you tell anyone you saw me, you— That's a *sin*."

Thunder didn't know the word; he stared at him blankly, then said in an uncertain voice, "I *must* tell. Telling about fringies is our way."

"Has anyone you know ever met a fringie?"

Thunder shook his head.

"Then you don't know your way. Make your own way!"

Thunder turned away, hating the man for putting forth an idea he could hardly understand: "Make your own way."

"To protect my country, I must tell," Thunder insisted. "When wheeled carts come to Tibet, we will be conquered."

"Do you see a wheeled cart?" the man demanded, sweeping his hand through the air behind him.

"But it means . . ." He couldn't explain how the prophecy related to foreigners' very presence, but he was sure that it did. "Are you . . ." Thunder knew what he wanted to ask, but at first he couldn't manage to speak. Finally: "Are you making maps?" he blurted as if the words had been torn straight out of his pounding chest. "If a fringie is caught making maps . . ." But the end of the sentence was too terrible to speak aloud.

"I am an explorer," the man said in a low tone, avoiding Thunder's eyes. "I've risked my life to save yours."

"My life," Thunder murmured. He felt his mouth trembling. But he screwed his eyes shut and turned away. "No, no, no." He pounded his forehead with his fist. "Once fringies know the lay of the land, they will conquer us." He felt blank with despair, yet more words tumbled out of his mouth: "But you look so Tibetan. Are you some kind of trader? They say fringies look ug— different from us."

"Son, calm down. Yes, I know that fringies aren't technically welcomed into Tibet."

"Technically welcomed! If anyone else had found you, you would have been killed at once."

"Then I'm lucky I helped *you*." He eyed Thunder long and hard. "I put Chinese ink on my hair and darkened my face. And I speak fluent Tibetan. That's why I can pass for one of you."

"And them?" Thunder asked, gesturing toward the other men.

"Mongolians. My servants. Look, I only want to tell the people from my country what it's like here in Tibet. Is that so bad? Have you never wondered about faraway places yourself?"

At that Thunder fell silent. Surely he had wondered about faraway places more often than any other boy from Chu Lungba. He wanted to ask the man all about the world beyond Tibet, but he feared that talking about such things would weaken his resolve against fringies. "The Ingi-li people—you're not Ingi-li, are you?" he asked. "They want to conquer us! Our village headman told us so."

"I am an explorer, I tell you. I take photographs. Do you know what those are? Well, never mind. The point is that I love your country." Looking down, the man added quietly, "I should have been born Tibetan."

Thunder was startled. He tried to imagine a person feeling he should have been born someone else. He imagined Second Aku suddenly feeling he should have been born Joker. Or what if his sister, Dolma, got it into her head that she should have been born in China?

Would Dolma begin struggling to speak a language she didn't know, bow in the Chinese fashion, and try to bind up her big boatlike feet into little stumps? With his chin raised he said, "You and your people could *never* conquer us. The gods are on our side."

"Conquer . . ." the stranger murmured, then stared at Thunder as if the boy held a sword against his neck. "My life is in your hands now, isn't it?"

Thunder looked down at his yak-skin boots. The silence was like a flock of birds rushing at his ears. He knew how the people of Chu Lungba felt about defending Tibet against the foreign world. The thought of leading a posse of his neighbors to this foreigner and watching them hack him to pieces was unbearable. He groaned, put his head back, and announced, "Let the sky know I will never report you to my village headman . . . or to anyone else."

The foreigner let out a breath. "That's a promise?"

"It's my solemn oath." As Thunder turned away, he noticed a conch shell, studded with turquoise and coral, near the man's pack of provisions. A pewter mouthpiece was attached to one end. Thunder had seen such conches before; they were used in the monasteries, or *gompas*, to call the monks to pray. Frowning, he pointed at it. "That's a holy thing. It should not be in fringie hands." Then he fled.

"Wait!"

Thunder turned to see the man holding the conch out to him. "Put it in a holy place," he said.

3

▼ ▼ ▼

THUNDER TRUDGED HOME with the conch inside his chuba, now and then stopping to lean against a scrubby pine tree and cough. His part of Tibet was unlike the desolate plateau to the north. Here the landscape was all gorges and barley fields and forests of juniper, willow, and pine. Signs of the storm were everywhere: downed tree limbs, a homespun apron tangled in a bush, an overturned plow. But today was breezy.

Like the other homes in Chu Lungba, Thunder's was a massive, nearly windowless cube of whitewashed mud bricks. It was two stories tall. The walls leaned in for strength, and from the roof's corners, prayer flags flapped in the breeze.

The ground floor around the courtyard was all

stables and barn. The family lived on the second floor, where there were three rooms along with balconies and threshing floors. These looked out onto the craggy mountain and the river racing down from the streaks of snow.

Snakes of smoke rose up everywhere, for all the villagers were burning boughs of juniper in their roof ovens to give thanks that the storm had ended. He sucked in the familiar and comforting aroma. Then, despite his weak legs and sore throat, he started to run. Thinking only of Joker, he swung open the gates to the courtyard. Inside, the chickens ran, squawking and flapping their wings, the horses whinnied, and the goat turned to look. The mastiffs barked, bounding at him, knocking him down. The bigger one sat on his chest, licking his face while her toenails dug into his chest and her tail beat against his leg. From there on the ground he saw Joker running to him, whooping, extending his arms.

"Thunder!" Joker cried as he ran. "Guess what, Thunder! I got you in trouble because you left me!"

"Joker . . ." Thunder struggled to sit up.

Joker flung himself on Thunder and the dogs. "But they forgave you when they thought you were dead."

In the evening, the whole family gathered around the hearth fire. They sat on the floor eating their *tsampa,* or barley meal, from the wooden bowls. The room was empty of furniture but held storage crates, wooden water tubs, and bags of wool. Bits of meat hung from pegs along with bladders of butter, strings of dried cheese, yak-hair ropes, ladles, and pots. Thunder's father worked the goatskin bellows with sinewy arms. Usually this was Thunder's job, but tonight he was too sick. He sat in a tangle of sheepskins and blew butter back and forth on the surface of his tea.

When the meal was finished, Joker and baby Razim played a peeking game near the green-glazed water tub, slapping its wooden cover down, then flying off into gales of laughter. Their mother, Nozim, got busy mending a chuba; Second Aku bit around the edge of a new boot sole to soften the leather. Thunder's sister, Dolma, a blunt-featured girl with a round chin, began preparing more tsampa by rolling it back and forth on the floor in a leather bag.

As they worked, everyone told Thunder about what had happened at home during the storm. They told him how Joker had tumbled down a steep bank while finding his way home through the storm. He heard what happened at home, too, when his father climbed onto one of the horses to go search for them.

Their mother slapped at the bag of tsampa as if to tell Dolma that she was not rolling it properly. "What happened to you, Thunder Boy, during the storm?" she asked.

"What?" Thunder asked, looking up. The foreigner's magic potion had worn off, and he lay with his head back against the wall. He felt achy. "I guess I slept, Ama," he mumbled. "When I woke up, I came home."

His memory of the foreigner was vivid: his round eyes and low cheekbones and the way he seemed to peer through Thunder's head to the back of his skull. It was hard to believe that the encounter was secret from all of them; he felt as if a bright picture of the foreigner were plastered onto his own face.

They asked more questions; he kept finding yet one more route around the truth until his tongue felt like a stone in his mouth. Still they leaned toward him, waiting, finally casting their puzzled glances at one another instead of at Thunder. He busied himself with his tsampa and would not meet their eyes anymore. Dolma gave the leather bag a particularly vigorous punch. At last they stopped asking questions, and only the trembling paper windowpane broke the strained silence.

Thunder woke in the night. He could hardly believe that he had been with a foreigner. What if everyone was right, and foreigners were practically demons? He touched his charm box. Praying for Lord Buddha to protect him against demons, he squeezed it tighter and tighter until, under the force of his grip, the box sprang open.

Out rolled a tiny bottle of the foreigner's potion. As it wobbled over the floor, it winked in the faint light and came to rest against Joker's face. Thunder was too startled to move. But Joker snatched up the bottle. "What is it?" he demanded.

"Put it down!" Thunder whispered. "Put it down!"

"No! Tell me what it is!"

His brush with the foreign world had been frightening enough, but now it hit Thunder how serious fringies really were. Fringies were about killing and being killed; even the stranger he'd met could so easily, so quickly be slain.

Thunder gawked at the bottle in his brother's fist. It was ghastly to have a foreign thing suddenly here in his own home. "Joker," he pleaded as a drop of the hideous potion dripped onto the floor. He leaned forward and rubbed and rubbed the spot until a little cloud of dust surrounded the place where the drip had been.

When he turned back to Joker, the younger boy waggled his tongue and held the bottle farther away from Thunder. "Tell me what it is, and I'll put it down."

Behind him Razim turned over in his sleep. "Give it to me," Thunder whispered. "You're waking Razim."

Joker only made a face.

Thunder turned and looked with blank eyes at his sleeping family. It struck him how vulnerable they were. If any of them awoke right now, their smiles would be there for him. Yet he had brought this demonic object into their world.

Joker watched him with a devilish gleam in his eye. "I'm making trouble," he taunted in a quiet singsong, then hoisted the bottle to his mouth.

"No!" Thunder lunged forward. "It's fringie!" But before he could stop Joker, the child had gulped the magic potion.

It was as if Thunder had sounded an alarm. Barely awake, the others were staggering to their feet. They all were tangled in sheepskins and rubbing their eyes. One after another, everyone turned to look at Thunder—Apa, Ama, Second Aku Tendruk, and even Dolma and Razim.

It was Ama whose suspicious words broke the silence: "So. You say you have been with demons."

Thunder remembered the foreigner's words as he held out the conch: "Put it in a holy place." And the trust in his eyes. He didn't answer his mother.

When Thunder looked away from his mother in shame, a chill passed through the room. Their silence accused him. "Demons? I drank demon juice?" Joker wailed, holding his stomach. "I'm sick! I'm dying!" Tendruk snatched up a yak-hair whisk and flung it down. Thunder's parents exchanged frightened glances, then both looked at Thunder as if he were a tiger, suddenly there among the sheepskins and quilts.

Ama grabbed up Joker, and Apa dislodged the bottle from his fist and recorked it. A bit of the magic potion was left inside.

Dead silence again as Ama fed Joker buttermilk from a yak horn. No one else moved; they just stared vacantly as she settled him on his sheepskin. Thunder felt tears in his eyes and throat, but he fought them down.

Tendruk pointed at Thunder with his arm fully outstretched. "Brother," he said coldly, "that one is trouble.

Always trouble! He loses Joker regularly. And how many times has he dropped his work to chase after the caravans? We must send him away!"

Apa's face wrinkled into a frown. But he said nothing, just went striding into the *chokang*, the house chapel, gingerly holding the bottle between his thumb and forefinger. After a few moments he reappeared without it. Tendruk was still standing with his hands on his hips. Glancing at him, Apa announced in a grim voice, "Tonight we think. Tomorrow we decide."

"Decide what?" Thunder murmured with a hint of panic in his voice. He was holding his eyes wide open so he wouldn't cry.

But Apa's word was always final. The others shuffled back to their sheepskins, Tendruk grumbling to himself.

It had happened so fast. While they all settled themselves on their sheepskins, Thunder stared at them through a blur of unshed tears.

After all of them seemed to be asleep, he crawled back to his own sheepskin and lay waiting for sleep, too. But he was tormented by the pain of his throat and the pain of his thoughts. He didn't know whether it was a demon or an evil emanation from the potion itself that caused him to creep out of his bedding and into the chokang. Against the far wall stood the altar of narrow shelves lined with eight small offering bowls, bottle-shaped tsampa dough called *tormas*, flowers, and sprigs of juniper. Buttered rice dotted with currants stood mounded on a metal platter. On the floor in front of the altar the bottle of magic potion lay on an embroidered cushion, close enough to the altar to neutralize its evil but not near enough to taint the offerings.

He inched closer. A soft leather bag lay with the offerings. Soundlessly, guiltily, Thunder worked a finger into the neck of the bag, stretched it open, and shook out a pellet of pulverized herbs wrapped in rice paper. It was one of three or four pills that Thunder's lama uncle had left for them long ago when he'd visited. Ama had never let anyone take the pills. "The moment will come when we'll really need them," she always said. Now Thunder let the uneven sphere roll from side to side on his palm.

Thunder put the pellet in his dry mouth, holding it on his tongue until it broke into gritty bits. Then he swallowed and waited for his throat to feel better. But he was dismayed. The pill didn't ease his pain; it actually hurt going down.

With his heart hammering, he knelt next to the pillow on which lay the foreign potion. He held it up against the weak shaft of moonlight and looked at it for a long time before chugging down all that was left. As before, his throat felt instantly, soothingly numb.

Eventually he picked his way back to his sheepskin in the other room and lay down. He stared bewildered into the darkness, and waited for sleep to come.

4

THUNDER WOKE BEFORE daybreak the next morning and remembered the previous night with horror. What had his father meant by announcing, "Tomorrow we decide"?

He crept past his sleeping family to the notched log ladder between the second-floor living quarters and the ground and climbed down, trembling. At the bottom he fled, past the clamoring chickens, through the sleeping village, and beyond, his chuba flapping around him.

He ran into the woods and sat closed up with his arms around his knees and his head down. His throat was better, but his misery grew worse and worse. He stayed through the sun's rising and all day while it crept across the sky, looking down at him in disgust. Not until evening, with his stomach completely empty, did he give up all hope and drag himself home under the three-quarter moon that hung over the trees like a glowing butter lamp.

As Thunder trudged through the courtyard, Joker came running toward him as usual. This time his face was wet with tears. "Thunder!" he called. "I only make trouble!"

"I've noticed that," Thunder said, forcing a smile. "But *again*? What happened now?"

Joker flung his arms around him. "I'm bad. But I'll be a good boy now. Just don't go away."

Thunder stroked his hair. "You know I won't leave you," he murmured.

Joker looked up, sniffing. "You will so," he said. "They'll make you."

Thunder's smile faded. He pulled away from Joker and plodded toward the house. He climbed the ladder and thrust his head through the hole in the floor of the main room. A shock went through him. His felt traveling cape was laid out on the floor next to a new pair of boots, his father's best blanket, two goatskin bags of dried meat, a brick of compressed tea bound in basketwork, and several of the silk scarves called *khatas* that Tibetans gave as gifts.

A shadow moved. Thunder saw that it was his mother, twisting a bit of cotton into a wick for a butter lamp. He opened his mouth to speak, then realized that if he could see her, she must see him, too. He stood deadly still, waiting, but she made no sign to him. Eventually he climbed up exhausted and sat with his feet on the ladder and his chin on his chest. "Ama . . ." he whined like a small child.

She stood turned away from him. "People believe things," she murmured as if she were speaking from down a tunnel.

Thunder clenched his hands.

There was a long silence before his mother went on. "Grandmother believes the rain is dragon's milk, though to me, that's a foolish notion. Second Aku Tendruk believes that to meet a person wearing old boots will bring bad luck. Come out onto the balcony with me, Thunder. Let's look at our village."

He stumbled after her onto one of the balconies. With wind on their faces, they gazed down at their valley at twilight. This sprinkling of sparse trees and mud-brick houses was Chu Lungba, barren, with rocks like the earth's ribs sticking out. A fire sprang up in a roof oven; at a distance someone chanted a mantra. Thunder knew every corner and rock of Chu Lungba.

Gesturing widely to take in the courtyard, the village, and the valley, his mother said, "Many believe that some people keep poison at a demon's bidding. When the demon tells such a person to feed someone the poison, he *must*. He cannot escape doing so. If there is no mongrel to feed the poison to, he must find a stranger, and if there is no stranger, he must poison a friend or a beloved . . . or even himself." For the first time since

Thunder had come in, she looked right at him. Her eyes were flat.

"I . . . know . . ." he stammered, pressing his hands together. "That's why Apa traded so much barley to buy new tsampa bowls for me and Dolma and Joker. Our bowls can neutralize poison."

"Though if a poison is not put into such a bowl but instead passes directly from the poisoner's hand to the victim's lips—"

Thunder felt as if he'd been punched. "Ama," he whispered, "you can't think I poisoned Joker?"

She was silent. He laid his forehead against the wall and closed his eyes. When he looked up, she was pulling, pulling, pulling the cotton wick through her fingers. Finally she spoke: "Soon the whole village will know that Joker is possessed by a demon. Once they know who put him under its power, never again will the people of Chu Lungba trust you."

"Possessed by a demon?" Thunder asked in bewilderment. "But I just saw him in the courtyard." Then, because her answer was too frightening to contemplate, he changed the subject. "Did the others all leave you alone here to tell me these things?"

"It's no coincidence that we're here alone, my eldest son." She said these words like a caress, and hope flared up in him.

"Ama," he said, "the potion *couldn't* have been poisonous because what Joker drank I also drank myself. And I'm not sick."

"Dorje," she said, using his formal name, "did a demon give you this potion?"

Thunder crossed his arms and stuck out his jaw. But she slapped her thigh. It was an old trick she had to show him that her patience had run out. He felt wooden and unwilling, and he hung his head.

"Answer me!" All his life she'd been commanding him this way, and he'd never once defied her. She flung down the cotton wick. He saw it fall, but he still kept his head down. "Is this how a son shows respect for his *ama*?" she snapped.

At that he looked up. He hoped that in the semi-darkness she couldn't see that his eyes were brimming with tears. "Ama, I took a vow of secrecy," he pleaded.

"No secrets from your ama."

"Please, please. I made a vow before the whole sky."

At that she sagged slightly and shrugged. "Your answer doesn't matter anyway. It's obvious that you met with either a demon or fringie, and one is as bad as the other." She narrowed her eyes at him. "Let's assume fringie. Why do fringies come here to Tibet? What do you think?"

"To . . . to see the mountains?" he asked, twisting a length of his chuba in both hands.

"Ha!" She spat words at him: "To destroy Tibet."

"But—"

"First one comes, and then an army. Thunder, even the Dalai Lama, that Ocean of Wisdom, will not allow fringies to enter Tibet. Is it important to our leaders that no outsiders see our beautiful landscapes? Open your eyes, boy! Fringies want to conquer us. They'll kill us to accomplish their goal. Were you with demons," she asked, "as well as fringies?"

He shrugged. His shoulders were tight and achy.

"I'll assume that your purpose for Joker was innocent. But as for the purpose of the demon that possesses you now, I know nothing."

Possessed by a demon! Thunder sucked in his breath. A hoarse, unnatural sound came out of him.

His mother stiffened.

Thunder realized she thought the demon had made the sound. He groaned, then thought: But a groan, too, she can misunderstand. What can I do if every sound I make only feeds her belief that I'm possessed?

"And why," she demanded, shaking a finger at him, "did you sneak into the chokang in such a secret and guilty way, after you thought we all were asleep again?"

He opened and closed his mouth like a fish.

"Whether you did mean to poison Joker—"

"*Mean* to poison him!"

"Or whether you did not, you must leave Chu Lungba now."

A shudder went through his body.

She wailed, "You would welcome demons and fringies, Thunder Boy." She took his face in her hands and turned it down toward her.

He tore out of her grip and stalked to the far side of the balcony. She followed him and held his face again.

He thought he would go mad from all her caresses and pulled away a second time.

"Thunder, the village council is meeting tomorrow about you. You must be gone before they decide what to do."

"Village council? How do they know—"

"Joker told his friend Mutik about everything that happened last night. Mutik's mouth is always flapping; now the whole village knows that Joker is possessed by a demon." She sighed. "At least they don't blame him. But they do blame you! The council's decision is bound to be bad. Look, your things are set out to go."

"Go where?"

"Never mind that tonight. Eat some tsampa now, and get a good sleep."

"Ama, *where*?"

"Tomorrow, Second Aku Tendruk will take you—No, don't worry about it tonight. To safety."

He covered his face with his hands. "I can't. . . . I can't. . . . There is nowhere for me to go. . . . I can't."

Even in the dark he could see that she was looking at him as if he were a particularly healthy weed. "All right, I'll tell you," she said reluctantly. "You must go to your First Aku Gyalo's gompa to become a monk. Someday you will be a lama."

"A lama? Me?" he asked, pressing the fingers of one hand against his chest. "I'm not fit to become a lama."

"None of us ever thought you would become a lama.

But every family should make at least one son a holy man, for 'Without a lama in front, there is no approach to God.' But this family . . ." She shook her head. "Your back is built to push a plow. I know that; Apa knows it, too. And Joker!" She sighed.

"There's Razim," Thunder said hopefully.

Ama shook her head. "Now that this has happened, it must be you. I have nothing more to say."

He tried one last time: "Ama, what if I go away, but not to the gompa? What if . . ." He appraised her, remembering how Tendruk had reacted when he mentioned becoming a trader.

But when he fell silent, she looked up at him. "There is no other way."

Instead of answering, he went to her and hugged her hard. He closed his eyes and stood with his arms around her. He knew that everything about his life would change now. No more for him a life lived in one tiny village; no more the round valley that cuddled its town; no more putting his back to the sickle until his body could snap. He would live in a place of straight lines and angles and stone, surrounded by people who wore burgundy robes and ate the same food and chanted with one voice. There would be people over him as his mother and father and Second Aku were over him now, but they would know nothing about him.

Gently she pulled away from him. "Your First Aku Gyalo is important; he's the governing minister next under the regent. You're lucky to be going to him." She pressed his arm, urging him back inside the house. "Sleep, my eldest son."

"Couldn't Apa at least take me, not Second Aku?" he asked miserably.

"Apa does some things, and Second Aku does others. We all have our place, you know that."

Bitterness flashed over him, but he played a trick on himself by hunching his shoulders and tensing every muscle in his body. It worked; after a moment he'd fooled himself into feeling only resigned. "If I'm leaving the family," he said sadly as Ama guided him toward his sheepskin, "then you must call Joker your eldest son now."

"You will never leave the family in *that* sense, so you will always be my eldest." She ruffled his hair as if he were little Razim. "Sleep well, my eldest . . . my own lama . . . sleep."

5

THE NEXT MORNING the whole family was up and busy in the courtyard before daybreak. Joker hid near the pile of saddles and blankets, gazing at the ground and only occasionally looking up with tears staining his dirty cheeks. Razim, dressed in a chuba that was too big for him, stood with a finger in his mouth and watched Thunder wherever he went.

They all wandered in and out of the courtyard, holding their steaming tea bowls. When Thunder realized that no one was going to speak again about what he'd done, that the whole episode was finished except for being rid of him, it hit him that things were truly beyond repair. He must leave his home. He would no longer cut the barley with Apa, chanting mantras as the two-handled sickle rose and fell. Next March he wouldn't be there to see Ama restart the growing cycle, scattering barley seeds from a shallow basket that, when Thunder sniffed it at other times of the year, reminded him of spring.

The family's voices carried in the thin air. He wanted to cover his ears to cut out their useless chatter and stomping feet. They were so noisy just when he needed silence and peace.

His legs felt tight and achy. With an effort he lifted one, then the other. If only he could question the decision. If only he could casually say, "I can make the whole village understand. I will stay."

But he couldn't question adults' decisions. He couldn't even speak of his feelings.

As they waited, Razim invented a game of showering Thunder with gravel, then hopping around him in a circle until he was out of breath. Apa worked with the horse on which Thunder would ride away. He took forever to adjust the saddle blanket, then at last bent to the horse's belly, gave it a slap that ended in a caress, clicked his tongue, and continued adjusting, adjusting, forever adjusting. When he saw Thunder behind him, he gave him a paper folded into a square, then covered with cloth and tied around with yellow thread. Thunder unfolded it to discover a charcoal sketch of a scorpion with flames in its mouth. He'd seen lamas selling woodblock prints like it as a charm against demons. But his family was poor, and Apa had drawn this one himself.

"I'm not much of an artist, Thunder," he said, "but when you get to the gompa, you can have your first aku bless it. And it will be as good as a proper one."

The morning air was sharp. Dolma said, "Smell the air. Oh, sniff the cold!" Her nose, moving like a rabbit's, caused Thunder to smile for the first time that morning. She jabbed him with her meaty elbow and said without smiling, "Good. I said it to give you the grins." Then she lumbered away and went up to the roof to make the morning offerings. From this oblique angle Thunder could just see the top of her head as she moved around near the roof oven. After a few minutes he could smell the burning juniper boughs she'd lit.

He followed her up to the roof. She knelt by the oven, fanning the juniper fire. "Dolma," he said, "I have a gift for you."

She turned, and he put the empty potion bottle in her hand. Dolma gasped. "No," she said, giving it back to him, her eyes frightened. "Apa wants it by the altar."

Thunder stuck out his chin. "But it's mine, and I want to give it to you," he said, pushing it back at her.

"It's fringie," she said, shaking her head. "I can't."

"Fringie means you must keep it secret. That's all."

"No."

"Dolma, it's all I have to give you. Besides, it has meaning."

"What meaning?" she asked, taking the bottle cautiously.

He didn't know how to explain and sat fiddling with

a juniper bough ready to be laid on the fire. After a few moments he asked, "Dolma, do you ever wish you'd been born someone else?"

She shook her head in amazement.

"If you did, who would you want to be?"

"Want to be?" Timidly she turned the bottle so that behind the cloudy glass the last drop of pink liquid rolled around. She looked up, bright-eyed. "The Dalai Lama!"

Thunder nodded. "This bottle means you can think about being the Dalai Lama. It means that—that you can imagine a different way."

As Ama appeared, climbing up onto the roof, Dolma thrust the bottle into the pocket of her chuba. She just had time to flash Thunder a private nod before Ama was with them, straightening Thunder's chuba with a gruff look on her face.

"Ama, can I go say good-bye to my friends?" he asked.

"No!" She jerked his chuba hard, the turquoise and cowrie shells woven into her braids clinking together as she moved. He let her go on smoothing his chuba, glad for his last moments to pass this way, with his mother coddling him.

At last Thunder and Tendruk swung away, wearing knives on their hips and white felt traveling capes. They followed the trail that snaked along the valley floor, riding in silence but for the clop-clop of the horses' hooves. For miles Thunder rode twisted around in his saddle; he kept hoping his father would come riding up beside them, calling him back home. At last he came to the familiar pile of a hundred or more *mani* stones—round rocks carved with mantras—atop the difficult pass leading away from his stretch of the world.

He had never ventured beyond this landmark; whenever he went out riding, his mother would call after him, "No farther than the mani stones!" Because they marked the confines of his world, he'd always imagined that finally traveling past them would mark a special victory for him. But now they only meant giving up hope that his father would appear.

They followed the road northwest, passing farms like their own, where wooden plows were pulled by yaks with tufts of red wool on their heads and strings of bells around their necks. Then they climbed into the hills, where here and there a finger of snow tumbled down from mountain peaks. Growing short of breath, they started the climb into higher mountains. Here they passed between them a Chinese pipe because smoking tobacco was said to prevent nausea and dizziness caused by great heights. But it only made Thunder cough.

As they traveled into the borderlands, they saw people different from any Thunder had known in his own valley: Chinese, wearing blue gowns and with long queues hanging down their backs; monks in saffron robes instead of the Tibetan burgundy; even Mongols, thundering past them on the fastest horses.

After several days they reached nomad country, a barren plateau dotted by occasional wild donkeys or herds of bison. Sheepherders and goatherds galloped down on them from their black hexagonal tents like big-bellied spiders with spindly legs. They demanded that Tendruk and Thunder buy the slabs of meat hanging from their saddles, and when they rode away, great clouds of dust rose, making Thunder's skin crack and bleed.

As they neared the gompa, the road filled with pilgrims wearing white gowns like fluttering sails. Some of them covered the distance praying on their bellies; one would lie prone, knock his head on the ground, rise, walk his body's length, and lie down again. This close to the gompa they passed occasional lamas, too: hermits with matted hair and leathery skin or fine regents, like the one who strode along while his attendant scurried beside him, holding a battered yellow umbrella over his master's head.

Second Aku gestured toward a mountain range silhouetted against the sky. "The gompa will be right ahead." For hours Second Aku had been proclaiming that Tharpa Dok lay just ahead. Yet it never appeared. Its doubtful site gave the journey a fantastic quality, as if they were floating into a dream.

Then, as Thunder started a game of pretending they'd never find the gompa and would go home, the clouds lifted from around the mountain before them.

6

WHIPPED BY THE wind, they sat on their horses atop the mountain peak opposite the gompa. Below them an eagle soared between two mountain walls. The gompa was a cluster of whitewashed boxes, each with a red band just below the roof and black frame windows. It clung to the cliff as if each box were alive and hanging on for dear life. The gompa was ornamented by balconies, zigzagging stairways hewn from the rock, ladders, rope bridges, and ramps. The many roofs were decorated with snapping prayer flags and huge prayer wheels turning in the wind. The golden roof of a pagoda crowned it all, with a cluster of bells hanging from each corner of the eaves. Now and then the bells sent out tinkling little peals.

Tharpa Dok was entered through an open gate in the thick outer wall. The arched ceiling overhead was frescoed with the Wheel of Life held in the claws of a snarling demon, and the gompa beyond the passageway looked like a village, complete with streets and open squares, houses and temples. A group of monks passed the gateway, their burgundy robes swinging as they walked.

Thunder stumbled into the gompa and his new life, passing rows upon rows of prayer wheels. He ran his hand across them to bring good luck, then passed a procession of boy monks wearing soft yellow hats, pounding hand drums, crashing cymbals, and blaring on copper trumpets.

Thunder learned later that the older and more important monks of Tharpa Dok had separate homes scattered along the gompa's dirt paths. Each had at least one novice living with him as a servant and student; more boys and young men lived in the dormitories that stretched down one hill. The monks worked for their keep as teachers, artists, astrologers, printers, accountants, cooks, and stableboys. Some were traders with exclusive concessions to sell one thing or another, such as tea, butter, or tobacco, to their fellow monks. Each one, whatever his status, received a portion of the gompa's income.

As Thunder looked around, he remembered his village of dull tunics, mud-colored houses, and dust. But this! It was colorful, with the monks' burgundy robes,

Buddhas of gold leaf, and enormous, bright paintings swaying in the courtyards.

They found First Aku Gyalo's house, one of four built around a sunny courtyard bordered with poppies. Tendruk pushed open the door. *"Ulay! Ulay!"* he shouted, using the customary words to announce one's presence. Unlike Thunder's dark home, this room was well lit by separate narrow sunbeams streaming in through eight latticework windows near the ceiling.

When no one answered, Tendruk went right in. An eleven- or twelve-year-old boy in a novice's robe thrust aside a curtain in a doorway. His shorn hair had grown out just enough that it looked like a tight, furry cap. "What do you want?" he demanded.

"Who are you?" Second Aku Tendruk asked.

The boy frowned but didn't answer.

Thunder bit the insides of his cheeks, wishing he could disappear.

Tendruk scowled, too, and tightened his hands into fists. "We're looking for Lama Gyalo of Chu Lungba. This is his house."

The boy stepped out from behind the curtain and crossed his arms like a village headman. "Lama Gyalo is my teacher. He's not here, so it's my house now. Go slowly," he added, in the customary way of saying good-bye. Then he spun around and was gone.

Second Aku began to scramble after him, but Thunder grabbed him by the long sleeve of his chuba. "Did you hear that, Second Aku?" Thunder asked. "The way he spoke his master's name!"

"I know. Most disrespectful."

"How can First Aku keep such a coarse boy as his student?"

Tendruk tugged his arm away from Thunder. "You don't remember Gyalo. Thoughts of loving-kindness run away with him. He probably adopted an orphaned street urchin. Remember this incident, and stop yourself from following in Gyalo's foolish ways." Then he strode away after the boy, leaving Thunder to admire the altar, the rosettes carved into pillars, the many sacred texts lined up on shelves.

Soon Tendruk reappeared alone. "The boy has told me a few things. He calls himself Gyalo's student, but I believe he's more of a servant. Or perhaps both. Anyway, this gompa isn't headed by an abbot, like some, but by a *tulku*—the reincarnation of the lama who founded the monastery. The ninth incarnation, or tulku, went beyond sorrow a few years ago. Since his death Tharpa Dok has been controlled by the regent, Lama Tsab-Chang, while they search for the next tulku. Last year two expeditions set out to find the next tulku. Both failed. In other words, the new tulku has yet to be found. So Gyalo is searching for him again."

"I don't understand. Do you mean I must go back home with you?" Thunder asked hopefully.

Tendruk set his jaw. "No!"

"Then . . . then should I wait here for First Aku?"

he asked, looking around at the house and imagining living there.

"Wait here? My brother could be gone for weeks—or months. Who can say when he will find the tulku, or whether he will find him at all on this trip?"

Thunder felt a sense of foreboding. He began drawing circles with his finger on the surface of the stone platform, or *khang*, on which he sat. "I don't understand," he repeated sullenly.

"That boy says this is *his* house while Gyalo is gone. And about having you, Gyalo's nephew, here, he feels—"

Thunder slapped his hand down on the khang. "Threatened?" he asked.

Tendruk looked at him with his hands on his hips.

"But it's *not* his house. And *I* am his teacher's nephew." Thunder was breathing hard. "And I'm older than that boy, too. Who is he to—"

Tendruk held up both hands to silence Thunder. "The boy says that until Gyalo returns, you should sleep in the gompa kitchen."

"Kitchen? Me? The nephew?" Thunder looked around Second Aku's house at the rosewood altar in the shape of a pagoda, the cloisonné vases, the scroll painting. Then he imagined sweating among the steaming cauldrons in the kitchen and the stench of rotting food. He leaped up and began pacing. "*I* am the nephew," he repeated huskily. "He's not."

Thunder glanced at Tendruk and was shocked to see

that his uncle's face was twisted with dislike. Then Tendruk looked away, hiding his face as if he realized he'd revealed too much of himself. "I think I'll leave now," he said, "so before dark I can reach that nomad camp where we stayed last night."

Second Aku's words hit Thunder as if he'd been slapped. He would let that servant boy uproot Thunder from his own uncle's home? Thunder clamped his teeth as if he might explode.

Tendruk stood up, yawned hugely and artificially, then started scratching the back of his head.

Thunder gripped Tendruk's arm and spat out in a fierce whisper: "You talked Apa into forcing me out of Chu Lungba. And you had to make me a monk. I could have gone to a dozen other places and done a dozen other things. I could have become a trader! Apa didn't know what I wanted, but *you* did. No, you forced me to come here. So I came. I did as you all told me. I never complained."

"Good for you," Tendruk said with a sneer.

Thunder swallowed, but his anger caught in his throat, as real as a piece of food stuck there. "And you *know* I have a strong back and strong legs"—he went on in panic—"but no brain. Monks are scholars. What do I know of studying? And now I am not even welcome in my aku's home? I must sleep in the kitchen?"

"You think too much, and you think too late."

Thunder's face crumpled.

"You know," Tendruk added, looming forward, "if I

were that boy, I wouldn't want my teacher's nephew here either." His eyes narrowed. "But maybe, with you gone, I'll have a chance at getting the farm one day."

"The farm? It belongs to us all."

Tendruk snorted. "It's my brother's farm, and if you had not come here to the gompa, later it would have been yours. There's no room for me in that family."

Thunder gaped at him in amazement. Then his heart hardened. "Will you get rid of Joker and Razim, too?"

Tendruk gazed at him calmly. "It will be easier managing them than it would have been with you."

"Why couldn't you have left me alone to become a trader if you wanted me to go?" Thunder burst out.

"Traders leave home only long enough to become rich and powerful. Then they come home and sell what little their family has, to make still more money."

Thunder felt a deep weariness flood over him. He found he had no more energy even to care. "You know I would never have done that to you," he said without spite.

"No? Then you are as much a fool as your first aku. You two deserve each other and deserve to live in this . . . this unreal place."

Thunder had nothing to say; he sat on the khang with his chin on his chest.

Tendruk started out, but at the door he turned. "The difference between you and me is that you sit and dream while I see what's real. And here's advice from a truth seer: You've come to the gompa for terrible and mysterious reasons. Don't forget you have a secret. And avoid making enemies—even of servant boys."

Half an hour later Thunder watched listlessly as Tendruk started away on his own horse, leading Thunder's horse and the pack mule they'd brought with them. Looking over his shoulder at Thunder, Tendruk called, "These days you speak too many words about your thoughts. If you have any sense at all, you will keep your feelings locked in here." He touched his chest over his heart, then clicked his tongue to be off.

▼ ▼ ▼

AS SOON AS Tendruk was gone, the servant boy sidled out from behind the kitchen curtain and stood gazing at Thunder with his chin raised. "You'll have to go now," he said.

Thunder dug into his pack and took out the tea bricks and khatas he'd brought as gifts. "These things are for my aku," he said. "Leave them alone until he comes."

"You'll have to go."

"I heard *you*. Did you hear *me*?" Thunder closed his pack and, though it was heavy, tried to toss it over his shoulder lightly. He hoped the jaunty toss made him look more at ease than he felt.

Alone and scared, he trudged off to explore the gompa, covering the grounds from end to end until he was spent. Only when darkness had crept in along the paths and alleys did he resign himself to finding the kitchen.

As soon as he pushed open the kitchen doors, heavy with iron bosses, the stench hit him. It was as if he were inside someone's mouth full of bad breath. The little light in the room came from three massive stone and clay ovens. Atop them stew bubbled in huge copper cauldrons. Planks lay across their rims; small bowls were set out on the planks. Ladders with brass-encased steps leaned against the wall near each oven. Countless barrels, churns with pestles, tea cans, and other vessels stood around the room on shelves. Knives and cleavers, iron hooks, ladles, and serving forks hung from pegs. Thunder could hear a constant low sizzle and got whiffs of the garbage heaped outside. Sheep carcasses lay under the table, and the floor was dotted with bits of food. The kitchen boys slept on the tops of tables, their shaved skulls facing Thunder like hedgehogs' behinds.

Thunder didn't know what to do next, so he noisily dropped his pack to wake them. At the sound one of the heads rose, the body behind it staying nearly prone. In the firelight Thunder could just make out a pair of eyes, dull with sleep. The boy they belonged to had a newly shaved head and ridiculous jug handle ears. His face was all rounds: round eyes, round cheeks, round chin. As he gazed at Thunder, his arched eyebrows rose. "Kitchen's closed," he mumbled, and curled up to resume sleeping.

Thunder cleared his throat. "I need to sleep here."

The boy looked up again. This time he managed to clamber around so that his legs dangled over the edge of the table. The legs were uneven; his left foot came only as far as his right ankle. Yawning, he looked Thunder up and down. "You're new at the gompa?"

"Yes. Well, new but temporary."

"Temporary?"

Thunder shrugged uncomfortably. "I'm . . . sort of . . . supposed to become a trader. Or . . . or maybe I'll be going home."

The boy's eyebrows rose; he was impressed. He slid down off the table and came closer, hippity-hopping because of his lopsided legs. "Then the gompa kitchen is the wrong place for you," he whispered earnestly. "We are the dumb ones here, you know. I myself am completely ignorant," he added, tossing his head as if he were proud of it.

"Anyway, I'm here now," Thunder said quickly, realizing that the conversation was getting away from him. He lifted his foot and kicked away a hunk of gristle.

"But why the kitchen?" When Thunder only grunted, the boy shrugged. "Always room for one more. Anyway, we'd better sleep now. The conch blows early to wake us—when the rooster is still putting his pants on." He smiled broadly, and Thunder was relieved enough to grin back.

"If you're going to be in the kitchen, I'll give you a word of advice: Watch out for Pounder." The boy shuddered as he said the name, then bounced across the kitchen on those asymmetrical legs and brought back a bag of food to Thunder.

"Who's Pounder? What's wrong with him?"

"I guess you'd say—well, when he runs into you, he'd rather harass you than leave you alone. Hey!" He held out a string of dried cheese, called *chura*. "Want some before bed?"

"Shut up, Seventh Turd!"

A yak-skin boot sailed toward the boy. He ducked, and it smacked into the wall. "You can have more if you like," he added, ignoring his tormentor.

Thunder glanced at the sleepy form of the aggressor. "Does he do that a lot?" he asked, holding out his hand for more chura.

"Who?"

Thunder gestured toward the boy who'd thrown the boot.

"Do what?"

Thunder shook his head, disbelieving the boy's density. "*That* sort of thing. Things to make you feel like a fool."

"Oh, you mean . . ." The crippled boy shifted uncomfortably. "'Make me feel like a fool'? What do you mean?" He looked genuinely worried. "Can one person put feelings into another?"

Thunder stared at him blankly. Was he stupid or wise? "Are you setting me a riddle?" he asked.

The boy chuckled. "Me? No. I told you: We're the

stupid ones, here in the kitchen, and I'm least important of all. I set no riddles. My name is Jigme, by the way. But I'm called Seventh Hand. Not this kind," he added, wiggling his fingers. "I have six older brothers, all here at Tharpa Dok. They give me things. My prayer beads came from my number three brother, Tashi, when he got new ones. Number four made me a slingshot. When the other kitchen boys saw them give me things, at first they called me Second Hand. Then they saw how many brothers I have, and I became Seventh Hand. Who are you?"

After Seventh Hand's long explanation the abrupt question took Thunder by surprise. "My name isn't interesting," he began, then remembered Second Aku's words: "You've come to the gompa for terrible and mysterious reasons." He found himself hesitating. Was it safe, he wondered, to tell Seventh Hand his name? He surprised himself by blurting, "They call me Dzo."

"Dzo! You mean like the creature that's half yak, half cow?"

"It's a nickname." It's a good name for me, Thunder thought, because there's no beast more stupid than a dzo. And there's no one more stupid than I am, allowing myself to be sent away from home, allowing myself to be shut out of my own aku's house. "Yes," he said, touching his chest. "Call me Dzo."

8

THUNDER WOKE TO the clatter of boys at work. He raised his head, blinking to focus his eyes. Seen in the light of day, the kitchen was one huge room, supported by red pillars. One boy kneaded tsampa in a copper bowl, his shoulders rolling with the effort. A second sat up on the plank that lay across a huge cauldron and ladled soup into metal bowls. A third came staggering through a doorway, wooden pails of milk slung from a yoke over his shoulders.

Seventh Hand was scrubbing something Thunder couldn't see. His bad leg was splayed out to the side, motionless while the rest of his body wiggled and worked.

Thunder sat up on the edge of the table and dangled

his legs over the side. With his head down on his chest, he watched the boys forming a group at the doorway. Each one carried two steaming tea cans. Thunder slid off the table but hung back, thinking them all so alike, nearly bald and in their dark red monastic robes, and himself so different, with his gray chuba and shaggy hair.

After a few moments an older monk bustled into the kitchen. Despite his bulk, he was light on his feet, tripping along like a snip of wool dancing on the wind. He noticed Thunder at once and stood looking him up and down.

"His name is Dzo," Seventh Hand volunteered. "He's going to work in the kitchen."

The kitchen master, Lama Thangspa, smiled distractedly at Thunder. "We have to go to the temple to serve tea," he murmured. "But you're a layman, so you can't serve with us. Make yourself useful until I get back." Turning to the others, he called, "Attention!" Though the group was already soundless except for the scuffling of feet, the kitchen master held out both hands, as if to magically calm a wild sea.

Thunder didn't know what to do with himself while the boys were gone; he dragged around the kitchen, looking into empty pitchers, lifting the lids off simmering kettles, heaving sighs. When the boys returned, they were dignified until the moment they crossed the kitchen threshold. Then they broke free and buzzed around Thunder like bees at a hive. They all wanted him to take over their jobs; first he did a bit of churning, then he was demanded at the oven. Next he hacked goat meat into long strips and hung it to dry for monks to take on their journeys. Eventually he was shunted into bringing in the heavy buckets of milk, unwieldy bladders of butter, and great sacks of barley. Sweat stood out on his forehead as he grunted and heaved. But when he finished at last and flung himself down on the floor to rest, yet another boy thrust his broom at him. So sweeping became Thunder's job, too.

By late afternoon, when the other boys left for another prayer assembly, the kitchen routine had numbed him. He dragged through the kitchen garden to the buttery and fixed himself a refuge out of the great cool bags of butter. Within this wall of butter bags, he stacked up half-filled sacks of barley that he'd lugged over from the granary. The blanket he'd brought became his pillow. He dropped down into his nest. The butter bags were piled high enough so he couldn't be seen if someone glanced in through the door. He heaved a sigh, grateful to have a sanctuary of his own.

Whenever the boys left now, Thunder slipped out of the steaming kitchen and flew to the buttery to collapse and doze. The barley's aroma inspired dreams of times when his whole family had bounced the grain in shallow baskets and watched the chaff blow away on the wind.

The day stretched into two days, then a week. The kitchen boys told him their names, yet he rebelled from learning them, as if that could prevent him from becoming part of the kitchen society. Instead, in his own mind, he nicknamed the boys he knew best the Big One, the Ugly One, the Vain One, and the One Who Looks Like a Goat. And of course there was Seventh Hand.

One or another of the boys constantly reminded him, "You must meet with the regent, Lama Tsab-Chang, to tell him who you are and arrange to have your horoscope read." But no one actually pressed him to go *now*; the meeting time remained vague. Thunder was glad. He feared the regent's questions about his home and why he had come to Tharpa Dok.

After their work was done, the kitchen boys sat around the center oven, toasting a mixture of tsampa and goat blood on sticks and telling stories. In the evening's half-light, it was easy for Thunder to pretend that this was his family hearth and that these dim forms were Joker and Dolma, his father and mother and uncle. The barley sack in the corner was Razim, asleep.

"Someone tell a story about Pounder. Who is he?" he asked the Ugly One one day. In response the boy only laughed without mirth. His expression told volumes: Pounder was someone to avoid.

"Remember the time Pounder killed that puppy?" someone asked.

"That was only a rumor."

"Well, I believe it. Dzo, they say he grabbed it by the

tail and swung it in a circle over his head and—"

"And it was yelping and . . . sort of screaming and—"

"Shut up about Pounder. He could walk in."

"And he flung that poor puppy over the cliff. It just sailed out in midair, scrambling and crying, and then it was gone."

They all were quiet.

"We called that puppy Dusty. Remember how we would feed it by the back stoop, and play with it, before it disappeared—"

"Do you see how Seventh Hand limps?"

But Goat cut him off: "I'm warning you: Quit talking about Pounder! It can do no good."

"He *is* dangerous," Vain whispered. All the others fell silent, looking around uneasily as if there might be a traitor in their midst.

Eventually, against Thunder's wishes, the kitchen life absorbed him. He lived in a world of steaming vessels and piles of grain, of the chop-chop of cleavers and the sloshing of milk. The gompa beyond the kitchen was serene, bathed in an atmosphere of meditation and stillness. But serenity had not penetrated here, where the boys earned their livings with speed and sweat.

Thunder felt pretty sure the kitchen boys liked him and was glad. Yet he knew he was different from them. While he dreamed of becoming a trader or of going home, they seemed to think about nothing beyond these kitchen walls, neither of what they had been before fate brought them here nor of what their karma would cause them to become.

For different reasons, Seventh Hand didn't belong either. A few boys lived to provoke him. If they teased him long enough, he could become so twisted, what with his bad leg, that he fell. One day at dinner Seventh Hand kept poking curiously at his tsampa, then cautiously nibbled at it and made a face. Thunder watched but didn't dare ask what was wrong; he liked Seventh Hand best out of all the kitchen boys, yet he realized that if he was especially friendly with him, the others would only start teasing him, too.

After Seventh Hand had pushed his tsampa away, uneaten, and left the kitchen, Thunder pulled it over, spread bits of the lumpy grain on the table, and combed through it. Only after some effort did it hit him that it was full of crumbled leaves.

He suddenly realized that everyone around him was snickering. He looked up sharply and saw that all the kitchen boys were watching him. Self-consciously he cleaned the table of tsampa with his fingers, put the globby stuff back in the bowl, and pushed it back to where Seventh Hand had been sitting. Without comment he finished his own tsampa, grateful that one by one, the boys lost interest in him and turned away.

Often Seventh Hand seemed to think—or pretend— that the boys teased him only from fondness. But Thunder knew how wrong Seventh Hand was. They sneered and mocked him because he was different.

In response to the boys' pranks, Seventh Hand would fling his head back and remind them of other tricks they'd played on him in the past and witless responses he'd made. Then he would flash a grateful smile when, laughing harder than before, they whooped, congratulating him sarcastically and thumping him on the back.

Sometimes Thunder thought that he minded their cruelty to Seventh Hand more than Seventh Hand himself did. "They badger you so," Thunder blurted one day. "Don't you want them to stop?"

"They tease me only because I hop. I guess I *am* pretty silly looking."

One day Thunder became aware that silence had fallen over the kitchen. Because he was the newest boy, he assumed that the strained atmosphere was directed at him. The blood rushed to his face, and he swept more and more slowly as the moments passed. At last he looked up.

But not one of the kitchen boys was focusing on him; they all were looking at one of the cauldrons that sat on an unlit oven. Thunder could just see the top of Seventh Hand's head. He was nearly hidden, sitting inside the big pot and scrubbing it so hard that it shook.

The kitchen boys were lounging against the pillars or big tables, glancing at one another. Some flashed triumphant smiles. A boy called Norbu tiptoed toward the cauldron, a finger to his lips while, in the other hand, he held a metal ladle. Thunder was amazed that such a lummox could move across the kitchen so silently, and he watched in fascinated horror.

Norbu paused before the cauldron and cast a toothy grin over his shoulder at the others. He swept his arm back, bashed the cauldron as hard as he could, then sprang away as the deafening clang filled the kitchen.

Seventh Hand leaped up, covering his ears with his hands. His face was distorted with agony. "Who did that?" he screamed, almost crying.

Thunder looked around for the kitchen master, but Lama Thangspa was gone. Of course, Thunder thought. The boys would never dare tease Seventh Hand when Lama Thangspa was present.

The others all were busy again, their backs turned to Seventh Hand. Thunder realized that he must be the only boy not warned to turn his back before Seventh Hand jumped up.

Seventh Hand wailed, "It hurts my ears! You know Lama Thangspa said you must stop!" But there was not even a lull in the clipped sounds of the boys at work. Seventh Hand shrieked: "I hate you! I hate you all!"

The boys answered at last with sputtered laughter.

Seventh Hand fixed an appraising eye on Thunder. He said nothing, but from his expression came the question: Are you one of them?

Thunder, gripping his broom in both hands, gawked back at Seventh Hand. Warily he thought: If I side with Seventh Hand, they'll reject me, just as they do him. But an unwanted image flashed into his mind of that first night: All the other boys slept while Seventh Hand woke, offered him chura, and told him how he'd come by his nickname. He looked at the kitchen boys' backs. Suddenly they seemed like the stupid ones, while Seventh Hand seemed as wise and kind as the Dalai Lama himself.

Thunder thought of the foreigner. He'd risked his life to help Thunder. He'd even said he wished he were Tibetan. He'd given Thunder his magic potion solely to help him and he couldn't have had limitless supplies: What if he needed that potion later himself? Presumably he would have helped any member of Thunder's family, any person from Chu Lungba, any Tibetan. Yet in return Tibetans hated him simply for being born outside Tibet. Apa and Ama would have eagerly slaughtered him if they'd been given the chance.

Then there was Second Aku, who hated Thunder for no reason that Thunder could help or change. Now here were the kitchen boys, banding together to hate Seventh Hand.

Why couldn't people stop hating and get along?

More than anything, Thunder wanted to turn around and walk out of the kitchen and never come back. Instead he took a step toward Seventh Hand's cauldron as the other boys watched disapprovingly and their spiteful whispers turned the atmosphere deadly. Thunder put his foot on the lowest rung of the ladder leading to Seventh Hand's cauldron and climbed high enough to peer down into the kettle. Seventh Hand stood barefooted, up to his ankles in gray suds. Thunder looked into his stricken face and held out a hand. "Do you need any help?"

Seventh Hand gripped the edge of the cauldron, his knuckles tight. He looked dazed.

Thunder dropped his hand. "Well, let me know if you do," he said, and backed down the ladder. The room, when he turned around, seemed unsteady. He looked at the other boys, one after another. Their narrowed and hating eyes found him guilty. But he stood before them with his hands in fists. If they wanted to fight, they could come on.

He went on waiting, looking one after another of the boys in the eye. But none of them made a move toward him.

After a long time, while the charged silence paralyzed the whole kitchen, Thunder turned back to his work. With his chin out and brows down, he swept in short stabs.

9

∨ ∨ ∨

THAT NIGHT THUNDER thrashed around in his sleep until next to him, Norbu elbowed him awake, then sneered, "No wonder you're named Dzo. You have yak breath." He shoved Thunder hard, and Thunder tumbled off the table and hit the stone floor.

He looked up at Norbu, smirking down at him over the edge of the table. Thunder didn't want to fight; he curled up on the floor and pretended that the fall had hardly awakened him.

The next day, working shoulder to shoulder with his enemies made Thunder nervous. First, out of sheer clumsiness, he spilled a can of milk. When the Vain One saw this, he kicked over a second can, spinning away before Thunder could accuse him.

And when Lama Thangspa told Thunder to help Norbu chop vegetables, the bully "accidentally" sliced Thunder's fingertip, then sneered, "Yak Breath, you're even clumsier than Seventh Turd. He's crippled—what's your excuse?"

Lama Thangspa shooed Thunder off to the medical lama, who wrapped his finger with sterile moss laid over garlic salve. Then Thunder dragged himself back to the kitchen, now empty except for one chicken pecking at barley dropped here and there.

Thunder sat down on the edge of the table and dropped his chin in his hands. So. He'd stood up to them. And from now on life in the kitchen would be a constant strain. He dreaded it and set his mind firmly: When the others were at prayer assembly one day soon, he would go to First Aku's house and demand to be taken in, command it of the servant boy if First Aku still had not returned.

Feeling some relief simply from having decided what he would do, he wanted to take his mind off his troubles; he needed to work. He heaved one of the big copper kettles up onto its side and swiped a rag across the gummy soot that covered the bottom.

"Dzo! Stop!"

He spun around. Seventh Hand stood in the doorway, his mouth hanging open. In each hand he held two empty tea cans.

Thunder dropped the filthy rag. "Stop cleaning? Why?"

Seventh Hand flashed Thunder a wan smile and shrugged. The tea cans, dangling from his fingers, clinked softly.

Annoyed that, as sometimes happened, Seventh Hand was suddenly acting stupid for no reason, Thunder shoved past him and went out. He could hear Seventh Hand's hoppity steps behind him and wheeled around. Seventh Hand bumped into him and stumbled back.

"Seventh Hand, what?"

Seventh Hand cocked his head, his smile vanishing. "I just wanted to tell you to stop cleaning the cauldron."

"Yes. You told me. I stopped. So?"

"Well, don't be angry."

Thunder sighed. "I'm not angry. But everything I do is wrong. Now even you start—"

"Stop. Listen, Dzo. You *must* not clean the bottoms of the big kettles. Because of Pounder."

"I know. He's a puppy killer." Putting his hands over his ears, he cried, "I don't want to hear any more about Pounder!"

"You'd better hear," Seventh Hand said grimly. "You see, he uses the crud on the cauldron bottoms. All the *dub dubs* do. Pounder's the soldiers' captain. Lots of them are our friends. Some were kitchen boys themselves. But Pounder is . . . different. You shouldn't do anything to draw his attention to you, or he'll say, 'Who cleaned this? The kitchen boys know they must not. Aha! There must be a new kitchen boy here. One who doesn't know my rule.' You see?"

"No, I do not see. What are you talking about?"

Seventh Hand closed his eyes, thinking. "It's all because he's a dub dub. They—" He gazed beyond Thunder, and his eyes grew large and unfocused.

"What is it?" Thunder asked.

Seventh Hand whispered, "Pounder."

Thunder turned. Coming toward them down the path was a lumbering giant with shoulders that swelled up under his robe. His hair was shaved down the middle of his skull but was long and coiled like rams' horns above his ears. *"That's* Pounder?" Thunder asked.

Seventh Hand didn't answer, but his expression spoke for him.

Pounder's robe glistened like ebony. Thunder learned later that he coated it with the greasy soot from the cauldron bottoms. That was why they were cleaned only after Pounder and his army of dub dubs had used as much of the grime as they wanted.

As he came closer, Thunder saw that Pounder's face was smeared with dirty butter. A stripe of cauldron soot stretched across his forehead.

When Pounder noticed Thunder and Seventh Hand gawking at him, he began to strut. A huge key was attached to a cord at his waist, and he carried a bamboo stave with leather thongs attached to one end, so that it formed a whip. Now and then he twirled it, cracking the thongs in the air.

When he reached them, Pounder flicked a hand

against Thunder's arm and growled at Seventh Hand, "So who's this?"

"He works with us," Seventh Hand squeaked. "In the kitchen, I mean."

"Aha! Kitchen boy, are you?" Pounder muttered, knocking Thunder's shoulder with the heel of his hand. "Belong to anyone?" Again he addressed Seventh Hand.

Seventh Hand stammered and spread his hands, explaining, qualifying, changing his mind.

"No tutor. No one." Pounder chucked Thunder under the chin, hard, as if he had rights over him.

Thunder reached up to rub his throbbing chin, then thought better of it and dropped his hand to his side.

Pounder asked, "Want to work for me?"

Seventh Hand leaped up onto his tiptoes. "No, he does not!" he chirped. "No, he does not!"

Pounder shoved Seventh Hand back, and the boy went down as easily as a tin cup. Pounder growled, "Let the dumb fellow speak for himself."

Thunder muttered, "I'm not dumb." He shook his head slightly. "And"—he cleared his throat—"and I don't want to work for you." He longed for the nerve to add, "Don't touch Seventh Hand again," but didn't dare.

"You will," Pounder warned.

Thunder felt the blood draining from his face.

Pounder started to swing away, then turned back to Thunder, clapped his great hand on his shoulder, and tightened his grip. Each finger was like a claw digging in, but through the ordeal Thunder forced himself to stare straight into Pounder's eyes. He hardened his shoulder muscle, terrified, yet sure he could make Pounder give way at least a little.

But he didn't.

Suddenly Pounder bellowed a laugh, cuffed Thunder's cheek almost fondly, then strode away toward the kitchen, slashing the air with his bamboo whip.

Thunder's eyelids fluttered down. After a moment he opened his eyes again. "I'm going," he said, straining for a glimpse into the kitchen where Pounder had disappeared. "I don't want to be here when he comes out." He started away, then put a hand on the wall to steady himself. "Who is he?"

"I told you: captain of the dub dubs."

"But who are the dub dubs? And why does he look so—"

"The dub dubs are the gompa army. They all look like that—the hair and all that grease. Have you never noticed the dub dubs training below the cliff called Broken Saddle? Running and wrestling and long jumping and throwing huge stones?"

"No."

"You'll see them now and then if you keep your eye sharp."

"I don't want to keep my eye sharp. Not to see him." Thunder touched his shoulder where Pounder had almost crushed it. He eyed Seventh Hand's mangled leg. "Seventh Hand, did he do that to you?"

Seventh Hand winced, pursed his lips, and looked away. "I . . . was so little," he admitted reluctantly. "It was probably an accident. . . ." Then he changed the subject. "Don't worry. Pounder won't come back this way. He always goes out the other door and stops in the garden. He loves peas." He shook his finger as he warned Thunder, "Stay out of his way."

"What did he mean, asking me to work for him?"

"Pounder recruits his army from fellows like you. You're big and strong and don't intend to become a scholar." Seventh Hand gazed at Thunder as if he were a prize sheep about to be slaughtered. "You're a kitchen boy with no tutor, after all."

Thunder clenched and unclenched his hands before asking, "Can he force me?"

Seventh Hand said quietly, "Dzo, I don't know."

10

▼ ▼ ▼

FOR THUNDER, THINGS had changed in the kitchen. He was sure that except for Seventh Hand, the kitchen boys had stopped liking him. Or if any of them did still like him, they didn't dare show it. Allied with Seventh Hand, Thunder was their enemy. Even worse, Seventh Hand had predicted that because Thunder was a mere kitchen boy, Pounder would keep harassing him until he agreed to become a dub dub.

Standing alone in the kitchen garden one day, Thunder said, "Let the sky know this," speaking a vow aloud in the Tibetan way. "This very day I am going to live in First Aku's house."

Once the boys had plodded off to prayer assembly, he flew around the kitchen, snatching up his traveling cape, blanket, knife, conch, and a few other belongings. He stuffed everything into his goatskin pack and was soon running across ramps, up and down ladders, and through stone alleys toward his uncle's house.

"*Ulay! Ulay!*" he called at the doorway. But when no one answered, it hit Thunder that even if First Aku Gyalo had returned from his search for the new tulku, he would be at the prayer assembly now, too.

Thunder went around to the kitchen and timidly pushed that less intimidating door open. Inside, it was smoky and dark. A few embers glowed under the tripod on the hearth.

With his heart pounding, he creaked open the kitchen storage cupboard, its door slanting off its leather hinge as soon as he touched it. From inside came the odors of stale air and rotting wood. Next to a bag of barley stood three tea bricks. Thunder had brought them as a gift for First Aku, yet now one brick was half gone.

A teakettle stood next to the hearth. Thunder stared at it. First Aku and his servant boy drink tea together, he thought. The boy lights my first aku's fire each morning. I don't do it; he does.

But if I passed First Aku, I wouldn't even know him, nor he me.

Still carrying his goatskin pack, Thunder left his uncle's house. He trudged back to the kitchen and arrived before the other boys had even returned from prayer assembly.

As he pushed open the heavy kitchen doors, he felt a touch on his shoulder, turned, and was terrified: there stood a dub dub. For a moment Thunder thought it was Pounder, for this dub dub, too, wore a greasy robe, a huge key at his waist, and a ram's horn hairstyle.

But, "I'm Seventh Hand's brother Tashi," the dub dub said. "You're Dzo, my little brother's best friend?"

Swallowing nervously, Thunder nodded.

"I thank you for your friendship to my brother. Some of the other kitchen boys pick on him. But not you." Tashi touched Thunder's arm. Then before Thunder had a chance to answer, Tashi was gone.

The next time Pounder came to the kitchen, snapping his whip as he approached, Thunder answered quietly as the dub dub questioned and threatened him. Thunder was resigned; he couldn't change anything about his life. Not Pounder, not where he lived, nothing.

When Pounder finished with Thunder, he lumbered over to one of the biggest cauldrons, flung it clattering onto its side, and rubbed soot onto his already filthy robe and face. After he'd sauntered out into the garden, after his stench had mercifully drifted off, Thunder relaxed against the wall and closed his eyes.

The summer shrank away. Thunder felt more homesick, knowing that the people of Chu Lungba were beginning their autumn work. By now all the families must be spinning and dying wool to make new chubas and blankets. His mother and Dolma were drying meat and mixing barley wine; the men were repairing saddles and sacks.

His father would soon take his last autumn journey, to the coal mine where he went once a year to trade butter and flour for winter fuel better than yak dung. In another few months Apa and Second Aku would be busy clearing snow off the flat roof of their home. But this year Thunder would not be there to help them do it, nor to throw snowballs down at Joker and Dolma whenever they turned their backs.

One morning as Thunder sat working in the kitchen, his fingers clumsy from the cold, a monk strode in through the big open doorway. Monks were constantly coming and going in the kitchen, to collect provisions for an upcoming journey, borrow a tea can, or speak to Lama Thangspa of this or that. Like the other kitchen boys, Thunder recognized the few who came often, and he glanced up to greet the man.

But as Thunder looked up at this monk, he froze. Apa! he thought.

In a flash he knew he was wrong. After all, his father was not even a monk, much less an important lama who wore a vest of gold brocade with an embroidered silk sash thrown over one shoulder. Besides, this man was strikingly tall, much taller than Thunder's father.

Yet he was so like Apa. He had the same features, the same sinewy neck, the same red spots high on his cheeks.

Then it hit Thunder. Here was First Aku at last.

The lama stood, an elongated silhouette in the doorway. The sunlight shone down on his shoulders. Even his hands were long and slender, like the petals of flowers.

When he shifted, causing the light behind him to glint, the kitchen boys glanced up, squinting and shielding their eyes. "Which of you is the son of Nozim, named Thondup Dorje and commonly called Thunder?"

Thunder gawked.

The boys shrugged at one another, murmuring, "Thondup Dorje? Thunder?"

But the lama was staring at Thunder. "Come, boy," he said, "I know from your features that you must be Rinjing and Nozim's son."

"Kushog, I am Dorje," Thunder admitted, addressing his uncle politely. His own formal name felt strange on his tongue after so many weeks of being called Dzo and then Yak Breath by the kitchen boys. Feeling shy, he made no motion to stand.

"Kushog! Call me Aku, son." First Aku strode forward to Thunder. "Dorje," he began, then looked around sharply at the gaping kitchen boys. "Walk with me," he said.

Thunder started to get up, then stopped. Something about the kitchen boys' expressions made him uncomfortable. He looked back down at the carrots he'd been dicing and didn't move.

"Nephew," First Aku prompted, "your karma says you must come with me. I will tell Lama Thangspa you are leaving." He strode past the boys into Lama Thangspa's back room.

After he'd disappeared, the boys went on looking at Thunder as if he were a slab of rancid pork.

Thunder wanted to say: "I can't help it that I'm unlike the rest of you."

But he couldn't.

Seventh Hand said bitterly, "You never told me that Lama Gyalo is your aku."

Thunder heard the reproach in his voice. "There are hundreds of things I haven't told you about myself!" he burst out. "And hundreds of things each of you haven't told me . . . or told each other! How can I think of everything?"

"Everything!" Seventh Hand said. "Being the nephew of Lama Gyalo is hardly everything."

"Are you going with him?" Ugly asked.

"Of course he is." Norbu sneered.

"Some things are all right to keep to yourself." Seventh Hand persisted quietly. "Some things are not. We are the dolts of the gompa. You let us think you were one, too. Even your name. The dzo is a stupid beast. But you are not Dzo at all."

When Thunder only gazed at him helplessly, Seventh Hand turned away.

11

▼ ▼ ▼

DRAWING HIS HAND through the air in a great arc, First Aku motioned for Thunder to walk out in front of him. As they left the kitchen, they left its smells, too. When Thunder had first begun to work there, the odors had made him nauseated. But that had changed. He was glad to go, yet leaving the familiar smells was like shedding his skin.

Aku and nephew started walking side by side, Thunder's pack bumping against his leg. His instinct was to fall behind, but each time he did, First Aku would glance back and wait. First Aku had a smooth gait. He kept his head erect and his hands clasped behind his back, as if there were much in life to walk toward. As they passed the place where the monks' robes were scrubbed, he said over his shoulder to Thunder, "Lama Thangspa told me that the kitchen boys know you as Dzo." He said it brightly, as if this were a matter of little consequence. But Thunder heard the edge in his voice.

"Is that wrong?"

"Wrong? I don't know. But it is not your name." First Aku fell back and looked over, measuring Thunder in a glance. He added after a pause, "You invented this name to use here, am I right?"

Thunder meant to ask how First Aku had found him in the kitchen. Instead he amazed himself by confessing, "Yes, I invented the name."

First Aku stopped walking and faced him. "Why?" he asked.

Thunder looked away from his uncle's intense face. He'd spent months yearning for the presence of this man. Now, standing before First Aku at last and being called on to speak, he felt like a dry husk. He didn't want to explain why he'd suddenly come to the gompa, why he'd called himself Dzo. But First Aku would squeeze the whole story out of him, he supposed. He hated himself for the way that he did and did and did what adults told him to do. He'd stood up to all the kitchen boys at once. Could he not stand up to this man, too?

When Thunder didn't answer, First Aku continued striding along with his hands behind his back. Thunder slogged along beside him, and the next time Thunder lagged, his uncle didn't even pause.

Gyalo led Thunder straight to the regent, Lama Tsab-Chang. His house had high windows that let in spears of light, and he sat cross-legged on a cushion at the far end of a dim chamber.

The regent glanced up. He was a frail old man with a stringy neck and pouches under his eyes. His translucent skin was covered with infinitesimal lines and crevices that seemed to blur his features. Behind him the separate cubbyholes of a cupboard each contained one Tibetan book made like a pack of cards, the separate parchment pages aligned between boards tied with yellow ribbons. In front of him a low table was set with a tea bowl, a bundle of parchments, a prayer wheel, and a string of prayer beads.

Gyalo bowed with his hands together in prayer position, then laid a silk scarf, or khata, over Lama Tsab-Chang's shoulders. "I present my nephew Thondup Dorje. I want Dorje to begin studying with me at once."

"At once," Lama Tsab-Chang repeated, his lip curling slightly. Running his prayer beads between his fingers, he jerked his head to show that Thunder must sit. "Any disease or deformity, boy?"

"No," said First Aku.

"Let the boy answer for himself," Lama Tsab-Chang said sharply, his eyes glittering. Then: "Are you a slave, debtor, or soldier?"

"Why . . . no."

"Does anyone object to your entry into Tharpa Dok? Your mother, perhaps?"

Thunder shook his head.

"Do you begin a religious life of your own free will?"

Thunder swallowed. He hadn't thought of his new fate in quite that way: "a religious life." It sounded so permanent. The men waited for his answer, and he eventually nodded, thinking, What else can I say but yes?

"Well, then." Lama Tsab-Chang paused, then asked, "Have you stolen, or thrown poison into a river or stones from a hillside to destroy animal life?"

Poison—again Thunder was silent. This was the last question he'd expected the regent to ask. What if the foreign potion *was* poison? "Not that I know of," he managed to say at last, his voice unsteady.

With a flourish the regent drew a parchment from a shelf behind him. He pressed his thumb into red ink and made his mark. Then he snapped his fingers for Gyalo and Thunder to do the same. One of the regent's servants held out a silk scarf identical to the one First Aku had just given Lama Tsab-Chang. The regent tossed it over Thunder's shoulders, then shifted his prayer wheel and set it down with a clink. A servant glided in through a side door. On a tray he carried a copper kettle loosely wrapped in green felt.

From the pocket of his chuba Thunder brought out his bowl. He took chunks of the butter offered to him from a bronze pot and drank tea with the holy men. The butter floated, melting on Thunder's tea, while he blew it from side to side. They drank their tea in silence until

Lama Tsab-Chang asked First Aku, "And the young tulku?"

Thunder glanced up in surprise. It wasn't until this moment that he'd thought through what First Aku's presence meant: he had returned from his search for the new tulku.

"We have at last found the next incarnation of Lama Samjam," Gyalo said. "It is only a matter of time before we bring him to Tharpa Dok."

The regent struck his fist on the low table before him. Neither man spoke for some time, and the silence had a tense quality that made Thunder dig his lips into his bowl and wish he were anywhere but there. He kneaded more tea, butter, and barley into a ball of dough while the lamas talked. Then First Aku was bowing, and Thunder realized the interview was finished. He thrust his empty bowl into the pocket of his chuba without even licking it clean.

An hour later Thunder carried the burgundy cloth for a monk's robe folded in his arms. On top of it lay an embroidered water bottle to be worn at his waist and prayer beads. They were made of smooth golden sandalwood; the attendant had first given him a string of rough black seeds, but after a few disdainful words from First Aku, he took that strand away and brought this one.

When they reached home, First Aku led the way through the master's entrance. "Zang-po!" he called toward the second room. A long pause followed before his servant boy slipped out of the kitchen. He avoided Thunder's eyes as he hovered near the kitchen doorway, his hands pressed against the wall behind him.

"Tea at once, Zang-po! My nephew has come here to live with me. Lord Buddha be praised."

Zang-po considered Thunder silently. Thunder picked up on the subtleties: First Aku had brought him in through his own entrance rather than the kitchen door Zang-po probably used; he had commanded Zang-po yet talked to Thunder with a fond and respectful tone. As Zang-po reluctantly started to go back into the kitchen, he shot an unfriendly glance over his shoulder at Thunder.

"Come here, Dorje—Nephew," First Aku said as he hurried, smiling, to a cupboard at the far end of the main room. With his hand resting on it, First Aku said, "I welcome you wholeheartedly, and I give you this cupboard to be yours, and yours alone."

Thunder gaped at the intricate design of interwoven dragons and phoenixes and the leather hinges. Unbelievable—a place all his own. Lightly he touched the cupboard as if it might bite. First Aku's ways were strange; Thunder had never had any place more private than the glade in the forest that he hoped none of the other village boys would find. Now to be suddenly given this chest . . .

He searched his heart for words of thanks but found none before First Aku had patted the chest twice as if it were a pet, then turned away. So Thunder said nothing.

But he thought: Here is a man to be trusted. I won't let him down.

Later, alone, Thunder opened his goatskin pack and began putting his few possessions inside his cabinet. As he knelt working, he heard First Aku leave the house. At once Zang-po scurried out of the kitchen. "Show me your things," he demanded.

When Thunder didn't respond, Zang-po grabbed at the pack. But Thunder reached up and caught his wrist. Zang-po's defiant expression didn't change, so Thunder squeezed tight.

An involuntary sound came out of Zang-po. It was a small sound, but Thunder felt it was enough; as long as they understood each other, all would be well. Thunder released him at once and smiled his habitual open smile.

Glowering, Zang-po rubbed his wrist. He paused before saying again, "Show me your things."

Thunder heard the cutting edge in his voice. He understood that he had not squeezed hard enough. Zang-po was still testing him. Thunder waited, hoping against hope that the boy would break into a smile. When he didn't, Thunder sighed. At best this boy was going to be tedious. "You can look in my pack if you want to," he said, "but there's not much to see." He pushed it toward Zang-po and watched while he flung things out.

When Zang-po plucked out his beloved conch, Thunder leaped forward to snatch it back. He thought, I forgot that was in there! I forgot!

Zang-po, seeing his reaction, held the shell away from him. But as he gazed at it, his mocking expression faded. "The spirals turn from left to right," he said.

"So?" Thunder asked.

"It is special," Zang-po admitted grudgingly.

Zang-po went on to inspect Thunder's knife. It had been his father's; the handle, of brass and horn, was polished from years of rubbing against Grandfather's palm and then Apa's and Thunder's palms. Zang-po turned the knife, caressed it, weighed it in his hand. But when Thunder said, "From my father," Zang-po tossed it aside as if it were chewed gristle.

This knife was the only thing he'd owned for as long as he could remember. It made him feel close to Apa. When Zang-po finally left to go to the kitchen, Thunder carefully laid the knife in the cabinet with his other few possessions and, smiling, closed the door. Things were going to be all right.

But when he opened the cabinet doors the next morning, he found the knife's blade bent and its tip broken off.

12

▼ ▼ ▼

THAT NIGHT THUNDER slept beside First Aku on the khang. When he woke in the night, he sat up, tossed some yak dung into the fire, and lay remembering that in the kitchen this was just about the time when someone would push him off the table. Already his life in the kitchen seemed far away.

When First Aku was nearby, Zang-po was always courteous and even friendly to Thunder. But whenever Gyalo was gone, he did what he could to torment Thunder. He served Thunder minuscule portions of tea and often spilled some on him. If Gyalo told him to take Thunder to one place or another in the gompa, Zang-po would lose him if he could. Later, with wide-eyed innocence, he would ask Thunder how they'd become separated as they walked.

First Aku welcomed each morning by reciting a portion of one of the Buddha's discourses. Thunder was supposed to say the text back to him in the evening. Though he earnestly tried to remember his lesson, he rarely could. Instead he would fall back on "Om Mani Padme Hum," the mantra every Tibetan learned in babyhood and continued to recite all his or her life.

Gyalo taught Thunder to read, too . . . or tried. One day Gyalo placed a book before Thunder on the khang. Like most others, it was about six inches tall and a foot wide. The pages, each a separate piece of parchment unattached to the others, had been hand printed from wood blocks.

Touching the book lightly, Gyalo asked Thunder, "Can you read any of it?"

Thunder untied the yellow ribbons that held the end boards in place. He scanned one page after another, biting his lip, pulling at his fingers, now and then clearing his throat. At last he pressed his finger hard onto a page. "These syllables are *yat* and *sen*," he said.

"Meaning?"

Thunder blushed, pulling his hand away. He knew the sounds that the syllables made, but not whether they went together to form one word, or whether each was part of the syllable on its far side.

First Aku took the page from him, reassembling it with the others. "Meaning 'marvel,'" he said. After that

First Aku rarely bothered to correct Thunder when he faltered over words.

Every morning and evening Thunder would leave the gompa grounds and go down the slope to the stream. The dusty earth was made up of grit balls that broke apart under his feet. He carried a water barrel on his back as the women of Chu Lungba carried theirs. Before he had come to First Aku, water bearing had been Zang-po's duty. But the boy whined to First Aku that Thunder was bigger than he and must take over the heavy job. At first Gyalo had ignored him, but Zang-po dogged him until he shrugged his consent.

Thunder didn't mind, though. Water bearing was a peaceful task. And twice a day it allowed him to escape from Zang-po.

The monks dipped out their water from a stream running off toward the village nearby. Thunder liked to scoop up the water right at twilight, though he could do this only when Gyalo allowed him to skip prayer assembly. As the vespers service began in the gompa above, he would stand and listen to the monks playing mournful hymns on short wooden horns and copper ones six feet long. When the wind shifted, he heard the villagers singing along with the gompa's tunes and smelled burning juniper.

Peaceful times like those, Thunder would stand and listen. I am a holy man, he thought unhappily. This would be a good time for me to pray. But he didn't know how. Pray! he commanded himself. Pray. PRAY! *PRAY!*

Thunder was filled only with a great silence.

But First Aku rarely excused Thunder from prayers in order to fetch water; more often Thunder and Zang-po followed their tutor to vespers. Gyalo motioned for them to throw back their shoulders and strut. They were not just anyone; they were *his* wards.

Prayer assemblies were held in the central temple, a building of burnt brick with the huge prayer Om Mani Padme Hum written across the upper story in gold leaf. This temple complex was a community in itself. Shrines dotted the outer court, each one dedicated to a different deity. Wooden platforms stood before these gods, each step hollowed out by pilgrims who worshiped by kneeling and knocking their foreheads against the board.

Inside, the assembly hall smelled of incense and old butter. Gilded statues were draped in brocade robes. During prayer sessions Lama Tsab-Chang sat, lotus fashion, before the altar. As his main adviser First Aku took his place on Lama Tsab-Chang's right. The monks sat facing each other in two rows on either side of the aisle stretching away from the altar. Thunder, the newest novice, had the farthest place down on the left.

At prayer assemblies the monks meditated, prayed, and recited in harmony with the bell and hand drum. The sessions were grueling. The monks sat with their legs folded in lotus position and moved their hands in stylized gestures to symbolize wood, fire, water, and air.

The rules didn't allow them to move at all except for their hands, not even to flex their toes.

On the altar was a statue of a golden Buddha sitting on a decorated throne with dozens of khatas hanging over its shoulders. An attendant stood ready to relight any butter lamps that went out. With his eyes open just a slit, the lamps looked to Thunder like so many glittering stars.

Thunder's place at the prayer assemblies was temptingly near a pillar, and he longed to lean against it. But Pounder and a few of his dub dubs always stood guard, flexing their muscles. If any of the monks sagged, one of the dub dubs would leap forward and, with the handle of his whip, crack the offender in the ribs.

Halfway through each prayer assembly the big side door would swing open. In would strut Lama Thangspa, followed by the kitchen boys. During the break between early meditation and mid-morning chanting, the boys would walk among the monks, pouring tea from cans into the monks' wooden bowls. One day, as Seventh Hand leaned over Thunder's shoulder, Thunder smiled up at him. "Seventh Hand," he whispered, but fell silent when Seventh Hand didn't smile back, didn't acknowledge him in any way.

That evening at sunset Thunder walked away from his uncle's courtyard and stood looking around, first at the high cliff to the north, then at the dust lands sweeping down from the gompa. He thought about winter. Snow would soon force people to stop their travels.

Many mothers of young monks would visit them for the last time until spring; traders would take last runs. In the winter all Tibetans stayed hunkered down at whatever hearth they were near when the blizzards struck.

Thunder turned to find First Aku standing next to him, gazing off, too. "Beyond that mountain, Dorje, lies our Chu Lungba," Gyalo said.

"Beyond that mountain and a few more like it," Thunder muttered.

After a pause Gyalo said, "Look to the mountain if you must, Nephew. But know that your life is instead like the river, flowing in a riverbed it did not choose and never given the chance to reverse its route."

When Thunder did not answer, Gyalo went on. "I have wondered, more than once, what brought you to Tharpa Dok."

Thunder was about to suggest that they go back inside when Gyalo added, "However this aspect of your karma fell into place, you are here now, becoming a monk. Have you considered accepting what Lord Buddha has set before you, even tackling the challenge of living your own life?"

"I try," Thunder burst out. "I attend prayer assemblies. I say my prayer beads, twirl my prayer wheel, I—"

First Aku held up his open palm. "All that is true. You are obedient, Nephew," he said, "but what about wise? This hushed and lofty place is not about the prayer wheel, nor about this," he added, lightly touching the prayer beads wrapped around Thunder's wrist.

"It is about this," he said, touching his temple, "and especially this," touching his heart.

Thunder grunted. But after a moment he held up his big hands, palms open. Flexing them, he said, "My life is meant to be about hard work and about a plow. Or—" But he remembered the fiasco he'd caused by telling Second Aku that he dreamed of becoming a trader. He didn't dare tell First Aku now.

"One day, when you are sure the assembly hall is empty, would you go there alone and sit? And listen."

"And wait for inspiration from Lord Buddha? I suppose he will reveal himself to me in a vision, and I will be moved."

"I ask you only to listen."

Thunder started toward his uncle's house. But Gyalo touched his nephew's arm. "Hear me," he said gently.

Thunder felt a sob coming up from deep inside him. He stopped walking and stood with his hands over his stomach as if he'd been punched. But he couldn't keep the sob down.

While Thunder cried, Gyalo stood very still at his side. Eventually the boy heard himself blurting out everything: about the kitchen boys and Pounder and meeting Zang-po; about his departure from Chu Lungba, fearing he had lost any chance to become a trader. He even told First Aku the worst truths of all: that he'd met a foreigner and drunk foreign potion and that the people of Chu Lungba believed he had tried to murder his own brother.

When he finished, he was rubbing a hand over his eyes and snuffling like a child.

A group of monks drew near and fell silent, wondering, but First Aku waved them away. Then he stood looking at Thunder, his hands clasped behind his back. Thunder's eyes felt puffy. He didn't want First Aku to look at him ever again.

At last Gyalo said, "The pill on your family's altar was one I brought? I don't remember. . . . What was it meant to cure?"

When at last Thunder spoke, he heard the hysterical note in his own voice. "I don't know," he cried, realizing it for the first time. "For all I know, sore feet."

His uncle was still gazing at the mountain. "Yet the foreigner presumably matched his potion to your illness."

Thunder felt as if a basket of rocks had been lifted off his shoulders. He said humbly, "I see your meaning."

"Foreigners know almost nothing about the heartbeat," First Aku said. "They hear only one pulse in the wrist when we know there are many. Is it their ears or their methods that are defective?" He shrugged. "On the other hand, we have given up surgery simply because an operation on an ancient Tibetan queen was unsuccessful. In fact, foreigners find surgery useful." He smiled fondly at Thunder. "In this case it is we who are unwise."

A shock of surprise flashed through Thunder. "You don't hate fringies!" he cried, suddenly admiring his uncle, loving him, worshiping him. He felt eager to prolong the conversation. "Aku, do you know about fringies? What do you know about them?"

First Aku smiled. But he only said, "Your mind has been opened to the foreigners' ways—or to one foreigner's way. That need not be a bad thing. It does not mean you must close your mind to your own beliefs and your own culture."

Thunder wanted to cry out, "You are wise!" But as he struggled to speak, exhaustion overcame him. He swayed and let his uncle lead him home, his arm around Thunder's shoulder.

After Thunder had slept briefly and risen, his sheepskin wrapped around him as if he were ill, First Aku asked, "If you were to meet a foreigner again, would you report him to the authorities?"

"Oh, yes," Thunder said eagerly. Then, seeing that a change had come over his uncle's face, he whispered, "That's what I should do, is it not?"

"It is a question worth pondering," First Aku said.

13

▼ ▼ ▼

AS SOON AS Thunder awoke the next morning, he pushed off his sheepskin and hurried outside to his uncle. The air was brittle cold; the landscape looked like a painting on glass. Seated in a patch of sun, First Aku was mending a torn boot.

"Aku!" Thunder shouted as he ran across the courtyard. "Will you help me find a way to leave and become a trader?"

Gyalo laid the boot and needle aside, then turned to Thunder with a look of great sadness. Quoting a Tibetan proverb, Gyalo said, "'Seeing the stars reflected on the lake at night, the swan mistakes them for lotus shoots, tries to eat them, and dies of hunger.' Must you, like the swan, chase after fantasies? Can you find no happiness in the real life that Lord Buddha has set before you?"

"Aku, it wasn't Lord Buddha who put me in Tharpa Dok, but my own stupidity."

"Nephew, even if I had the ability to help you accomplish your goal, I would find it hard to decide whether to do so." He picked up the boot and needle again and continued to work. "But as things stand, I am saved the torment that such a dilemma would cause me. To put it simply, I have absolutely no resources that could help you shift toward the life of a trader."

Thunder scrambled down to sit beside his uncle on the courtyard stones. "Aku, doesn't scripture teach, 'Be not aimless, like the flitting hummingbird. Instead be the eagle, flying straight to the goal by devoting yourself completely!'"

First Aku threw his head back and laughed. "Nephew," he said, catching his breath, "you have learned to speak my own language to me. Perhaps we should put aside our burdens more often and speak with each other as aku and nephew, as person and person, as soul and soul."

Thunder straightened up, beaming.

"Yet I wonder about your meaning," First Aku said. "Why do you despise your life here? Is it Zang-po? You must find him a thorn pricking you."

Thunder lifted his hands, then let them drop.

"It is often hard for you to find words," First Aku said, his head tilted to one side as around them the autumn wind puffed up cloudlets of dust. He eyed Thunder for a long time before asking, "Have you wondered why I keep Zang-po here with me? He is a thorn in my side, too, with all his selfish ways. But living with him tests my compassion. No doubt you find me naive about Zang-po. But remember, I have no son. Perhaps I *wish* to be naive." He sighed. "Zang-po feels you have taken his place, and I suppose you have. But try to understand his anger. In time you two will feel bound together like brothers."

"Aku, that will never be."

"With understanding will come compassion. This is always the way." First Aku began sewing again.

"I don't want the compassion of a monk," Thunder muttered sullenly. "I want the courage of a trader."

"Ah, courage." First Aku placed both hands on his knees and gazed forward. Thunder laid his cheek on his knees and watched him.

First Aku turned from his vision and looked at Thunder. "Courage. But what is courageous about a trader's life, Nephew?"

Thunder lifted his head. "Exotic places," he said, "and facing bandits. And crossing the great plateau and running out of water and food . . . and no shelter. And windstorms and barely living through it all—" He sat up on his knees. "And even the big city, Lhasa!"

"Nephew"—Gyalo chuckled—"I love seeing your eyes shine as you imagine these things."

Thunder nodded eagerly. Except for First Aku, no

adult had ever allowed him to speak of his hopes and dreams and the workings of his own mind. Even talking about becoming a trader felt like a step toward his goal.

In time First Aku went on speaking. His tone was soothing as he told Thunder, "The trader's life *is* one of adventure. But adventure is not the same as courage. Which do you seek? Real courage lies here at the gompa, where in our meditation sessions we absorb the pain of the world's karma in our own aching bodies, where we struggle to live harmoniously with the likes of Zang-po, where—"

"Aku, to me, the trader's life is one of *both* adventure and courage. Meditation!" He scoffed, dismissing it with the brush of a hand. "I don't help anyone by meditating. When I meditate, I think about . . . I don't even know."

"You daydream."

"I remember home, and the kitchen, and I . . ." His voice fell away.

"But there is another way." Gyalo smoothed the mended boot and laid it to one side. "Nephew," he said, "if you wish to give up this life and give up your family—"

"But already I have given up my family," Thunder said, then saw the slight stiffening of First Aku's cheek and felt a shock of realization. He bowed his head. "I'm . . . sorry, Aku," he said. "Here, at the gompa, of course I am with family."

Gyalo searched Thunder's face. There was nothing of frailty in Gyalo's expression, so when the thought flashed into Thunder's mind that Aku was vulnerable, he forced it down.

"Nephew, there are more ways than one to live your life—for any of us to live our lives."

Thunder looked sidelong at First Aku, reluctant to turn and show his whole face.

"But," First Aku added gently, "my words are from *my* heart, not yours. You must find your own karma."

Thunder shot him a quick glance of surprise. "But how do I find my karma?"

"By making choices."

Thunder sat back on his heels, amazed. Never had anyone suggested that his life could be about choices. "I make choices myself?" he asked haltingly, his fingertips pressed against his chest. Images sprang up in his mind, of his ama saying, "You must leave Chu Lungba," and later, of Second Aku saying, "You think too late." It hit Thunder that all his life other people had been telling him what he must do.

A mournful lowing sound floated out over the wide sky and reached him. He looked up at the temple roof. A young monk stood silhouetted there, holding up to his mouth a conch horn like Thunder's own. First Aku had not answered his question, but Thunder didn't press him. "Aku," he said instead, pointing up toward the monk, "do you hear that?"

"The conch calling us? Of course I do."

"I remember hearing it when I first came here. But I haven't noticed the sound for many weeks," Thunder said, leaning back, letting the drone wash over him like a lament.

First Aku smiled gently. "You hear it now," he said. He tipped his face up to the sky as his nephew's face was tipped up, and listened with him.

14

∨ ∨ ∨

MID-MONTH DAY was auspicious in any month. But it was especially lucky this month, for that night the moon would be full. Even better, Tharpa Dok's tulku would arrive then.

First Aku was excited, and so were monks all over the gompa as they prepared for the child's arrival. From the treasure house over the temple they brought down gold bowls, incense burners, carpets, satin wall hangings, cloisonné vases, and illuminated manuscripts. Master artists created banners and frescoes commemorating the tulku in his previous lives.

Thunder peeked through the doors of the Moon Temple, where dancers practiced hour after hour for the celebration to be held on the day of the tulku's arrival. The young dancers spun sticks around their fingers as they swayed; their handbells tinkled, and drums thumped.

Those monks who already had formal satin and silk clothes brought them out for the enthronement ceremony. First Aku gave Thunder and Zang-po new robes, Thunder's of red and yellow silk with wide sleeves that dangled below his fingertips.

Finally the whirlwind of arrangements wound down, and on mid-month day, First Aku, Thunder, and Zang-po rose early and hurried to the dining hall of the *khamstan*, or dormitory, where they often ate. Like them, the other monks wore their festive costumes and the unique hats that designated their religious specialties. Thunder's was like those of the other novices, a cap with a forward-thrusting plume like a rooster's comb. The hermits who had come down from grottoes in the cliffs wore pointed helmets; adepts in meditation had on broad hats with scalloped decorations; government officials' hats were wide-brimmed with low crowns.

In the khamstan dining hall Thunder pressed through the throng toward the cauldron of tsampa at the front. As he started his meal, other monks were already hurrying to meet the tulku's caravan. Thunder wolfed down his tsampa and followed the others outside. Ahead of him the monks chattered as they strode against the cold wind, past the gompa gate to the track leading down toward the stream.

Near the edge of the gompa grounds, the monks,

pilgrims, and villagers fanned out to await the tulku. Standing in little groups, they gazed at the desolate landscape of rock and dust that swept down from Tharpa Dok. They carried yellow or blue umbrellas and bright banners that snapped in the cold wind. These splashes of color kept jerking around as the people shifted to get a better view of the road.

Musicians waited farthest along the route, where they could announce the tulku's arrival to the others. Their thighbone trumpets and long copper horns lay beside them in the sparse grass. Nearby, a few of the youngest monks stood holding gifts to pass up to the five-year-old tulku as he went by in his palanquin. One child held a Chinese snuffbox, another a plate of candied dates. Now and then the little boys would set down their gifts, jump in place, and blow on their hands to stay warm.

They waited. The crisp air was motionless now, the wind too weak even to stir the hem of a robe. Thunder rubbed his cold arms in an effort to rouse himself, then relapsed into sleepily staring at nothing.

Thunder suddenly realized that the group of monks off to one side was the kitchen boys. Seventh Hand stood apart from them as usual, shivering and forlorn as he gazed down the path. Thunder watched him, wishing he could speak with his onetime friend. But he felt too shy and turned away, then turned back. If I tell myself I am taking just one step and don't think about where I'm going, he thought, I can do this.

So he took one step. And by the time he neared Seventh Hand he'd found courage, and he ran the last few steps with his arms open. "Seventh Hand!" he crowed, paying no attention to the other kitchen boys as they muttered and sidled away.

Seventh Hand turned to him. His mouth dropped open in surprise. "Have you eaten, Thondup Dorje, son of Nozim?" he asked stiffly, using the formal Tibetan greeting.

"Don't call me by that stuffy name, old friend," he said, leaning forward to touch foreheads.

"What do they call you, if not Thondup Dorje, son of Nozim? Surely not Dzo?"

Thunder laughed. "One name is as good as another. Dzo is all right. Or Thunder. My family calls me Thunder. You call me that, too."

"I prefer to call you Dorje if you do not object."

Thunder's smile faded. "I see," he said softly, and straightened up. He stood looking at Seventh Hand. When he had known him in the kitchen, Thunder had thought of his friend's face as a study in joy, the way his big upper lip perched on the smaller lower one and his round eyes turned to half-moons when he laughed. How could such a silly face know distress? Yet now it did; Seventh Hand's forehead was contracted, his mouth down.

Thunder tried again. "It's good to see you."

Seventh Hand didn't smile; he only looked sidelong at Thunder as if he didn't trust him.

"I think of you all the time—you and your flappers." Thunder teased him fondly, touching one of Seventh Hand's big ears.

But once Thunder stopped speaking, the silence seemed loud. They both shifted nervously and turned to look down the path as around them the wind picked up again and whipped at their robes.

Thunder glanced at Seventh Hand, and it struck him that he'd been a fool even to try. He spun around to walk away, but behind him Seventh Hand burst out, "You only pretended to be a kitchen boy. Really you are the important nephew of—"

"Why do you speak as if I were the Dalai Lama himself?" Thunder flashed back at him. "Are we no longer friends?"

"Friends? You and I? Of course not!"

So it had been a mistake to come talk to him. Thunder turned away again and, with his arms crossed, started back to where he'd stood before. But he heard Seventh Hand coming after him and looked back one more time. Thunder had always construed Seventh Hand's uneven walk as a happy little hippity-hop. But as he watched the kitchen boy, he realized that Seventh Hand bounced only because he was lame. Thunder said bitterly, "We were friends. You gave me chura. I stood up for you."

"But I would never have offered you chura if I'd known who you were."

"You would have let me starve?"

"Starve?" Seventh Hand murmured, shaking his head in confusion. "I would never have been so presumptuous as to give you chura right from the sack. I would have said, 'Go where you belong! I'm not worthy!'"

Thunder turned his face away as if he'd been slapped. "Presumptuous . . ." he said slowly. "Is that why you never speak or even smile at me when you pour my tea at prayer assemblies? Because that would be presumptuous?"

"Of course. I misunderstood. I thought we were equals and could be friends. But if we're not equals, then being friends is not the way."

Thunder gazed at a beetle lying upside down near his foot. It thrashed around aimlessly, rocking on its round back. It would never right itself without help. Thunder knelt, took it into his hand, and sent it lumbering off.

Seventh Hand spoke. "Maybe you don't realize how important your aku is?"

"I realize."

The light went out of Seventh Hand's eyes. He turned and started toward the other kitchen boys, then cast a last, puzzled look over his shoulder at Thunder. "I meant no harm."

Thunder trudged back to where he'd been standing before and stared at that point on the horizon where the tulku's caravan was expected to appear. He grew so bored with waiting that his eyes glazed over and he scarcely cared whether the gompa ever had a tulku again.

But when it seemed that the child would never arrive, the procession appeared at last as bright spots of red, yellow, and blue splashed against the dull earth and gray sky. As the distant caravan snaked along, the gompa musicians crashed their cymbals and blared their horns.

Soon the procession—yaks, donkeys, and the rocking palanquin itself—began clambering up out of the far gorge. As it neared him, everyone bowed his head over his prayer beads or prayer wheel. All Thunder could hear over the monks' chanting was the creaking of the wooden saddles and shifting packs and the rhythmic thudding of hooves on the dirt path.

Only after the procession had passed by did Thunder dare look up and watch it wind away toward the gompa. Now and then, from within the golden palanquin, the face of a small boy would flash forth, then disappear.

First Aku, a member of the official greeting party, bustled off with a wink and fond pat on the shoulder for Thunder.

As Thunder stood alone, Zang-po came up from behind and jabbed him in the ribs. "Come with me."

"Leave me alone," Thunder said, jerking away, and Zang-po strode off. Thunder stayed where he was, watching everyone hurrying and smiling. But he didn't want to trail after those who were dogging the caravan, and eventually he started home.

As Thunder turned the first corner on his route home, he saw Zang-po, looking annoyed, waiting for him. As soon as he saw that Thunder was indeed following, he smiled slightly, then shot forward and out of sight again. Thunder plodded after him with his head down, walking more and more slowly as he neared First Aku's house.

Thunder pushed open the door. Zang-po was kneeling in the corner near the altar, scrabbling at the brickwork. As Thunder stood watching in silence, Zang-po leaped up, swearing, ran into the kitchen, and came back with a rock. He used it to continue chipping away at the bricks. After finishing with the rock, Zang-po glanced over his shoulder at Thunder. "Watch for him," he ordered. "If he catches us, you'll be in big trouble."

"Not I."

"Yes, you."

"I won't watch for him," Thunder muttered, and sat down on the floor beside his own cabinet.

"Here it is!" Zang-po crowed at last, and reluctantly Thunder turned around to see. Zang-po dragged a metal box out from behind one of the bricks. It scraped noisily as it slid out. After blowing the dust off it, he pried open the lid. Inside lay fifteen or more of the precious necklaces, called *gul-gyan*, that formed the most valuable portion of a wealthy woman's dowry and were the most cherished of all Tibetan jewelry.

Zang-Po's grin was triumphant, and his eyes shone as he held up a necklace for Thunder to admire. The beads glimmered, and Thunder leaned forward, impressed in spite of himself. "Gorgeous," Zang-po murmured. His eyelids fluttered as he rubbed the beads against his own cheek. "The turquoise . . . the gold. The coral is like the inside of a baby's ear . . . No!" he cried, snatching back a necklace as Thunder reached for it.

As he gazed at the beads, Thunder's stomach lurched. He felt almost sick but didn't know why. He asked slowly, "So?"

"So?" Zang-po mimicked. "So how do you think your cherished aku came by these treasures?"

"Are they Aku's then?" Thunder asked. He knew that the question was stupid. He wanted to be stupid.

"'Are they Aku's then?'" Zang-po mocked in a singsong.

Suddenly Thunder spoke with passion: "I want no part in this. I'm going out."

"You stay here," Zang-po commanded. "You listen to me. How do you think your aku got these?"

"I don't know."

"He got them by making sure *he* is the one who reads scripture at any wealthy woman's funeral—if he expects her funeral expenses to be paid with her gulgyan, that is. Of course he's supposed to give the gulgyan to the gompa treasury. But Lama Gyalo doesn't always give them up. He surrenders the necklaces that aren't so valuable, so no one will suspect what he's up to. Sometimes, though . . . These are beauties."

"I don't believe you."

Zang-po glanced at Thunder, opened his mouth to speak, then shrugged. He replaced the gul-gyan in the metal box, one necklace after another. He positioned each one in precisely the same order in which he'd removed it. When he'd finished hiding the box in the recess, Thunder could not have guessed which brick concealed it. He didn't *want* to know which brick hid the box, didn't want even to know the box existed. He only wanted to turn back time to when First Aku had still been his hero.

15

▼ ▼ ▼

FEELING GLUM, THUNDER plodded along the gompa paths. He hardly noticed when he joined the end of the procession of people braving the wind to reach the cliffside Temple of the Oracle. Dondrub was about to prophesy about the new tulku.

Turning his face away from the slashing wind, Thunder struggled up the rough-hewn staircase to hear what Dondrub would say. The final stairs were carved out of the cliff and painted a riot of spirals and demons and gods. They were flanked by two tin lions. Beyond them stood the Temple of the Oracle, surrounded by scarlet pillars festooned with colorful banners and scrolls. Bits of rusted armor hung on the temple columns along with chain-mail coats and bows with arrows in leather quivers. A gallery enclosed the court-yard on two sides. In the gloomy corridor underneath, Thunder could make out the nightmarish frescoes of monsters and headless birds, beasts with three eyes, and claws that dripped blood. Flags and streamers printed with magical spells dangled from ropes stretched overhead.

In the temple courtyard the throng buzzed, every-one jostling and nudging his way to a better view. Most of the Tharpa Dok monks were in the oracle's audience, and many villagers and pilgrims were there, too. Pounder and his dub dubs kept order by swinging straw-stuffed leopard skins at the crowd and by blow-ing on thighbone trumpets.

Thunder felt a hand on his forearm and looked around, startled, into First Aku's face. "Quickly, Nephew," Gyalo said, gesturing toward one of the demons painted on the wall. "Dondrub's protective spir-it just pushed down one of the guards. Obviously it is warning us that the guard must not participate in the ceremony. Come take his place."

Thunder shrank back, overcome with shyness and distrust as he remembered his uncle's stolen gul-gyan. "I don't want to," he begged.

But Gyalo dragged him forward. "You must! Nephew, please!"

"I really don't—" Thunder said, but First Aku was pulling hard on his arm. Reluctantly Thunder let his uncle drag him through the brass doors and into the temple's dark chamber. It was lit only by the sacred fire; on the wall above the blaze hung a painting of the ferocious three-headed monster that possessed the oracle, Dondrub, when he had his fits. In the flickering firelight the monster seemed to be alive.

A huge guard stepped out of the shadows and held out to Thunder a silk dragon cloak on which a green serpent snaked down from the left shoulder to where it snarled on the chest. Thunder was so overwhelmed by the garment that it took him a moment to recognize the guard who held it out to him: Pounder, coldly staring at him.

Fearfully Thunder shrugged on the cloak. His hands shook as he tied the brocade sash. Then, shoulder to shoulder with his oppressor, he had to step up to the brass doors, fling them open, and march out.

As they went out into the cold courtyard, other attendants were carrying the new tulku, seated on his snow leopard throne, up the last few stairs and into Dondrub's courtyard. After they had positioned the child in front of the temple's massive doors, Lama Tsab-Chang took his place behind the tulku and set a claw-like hand on the child's shoulder. Thunder remembered meeting Lama Tsab-Chang the day Thunder had moved from the kitchen to First Aku's house. Like that time, today the regent had a sour look on his ancient and waxy face. In front of him the tulku sat innocent and expectant, looking around as he kicked his feet forward and back.

A hush settled over the courtyard. Then a bloodcurdling screech. Dondrub leaped out from his chamber. He wore a silver headdress decorated with tufts of wool and a breastplate over his green and gold dragon cloak. A polished steel mirror hung around his neck. It flashed as he whirled past Thunder and Pounder into the middle of the courtyard. His chest heaved; his lips were drawn back in a snarl. The crowd shrank back, hissing. Chills ran up Thunder's spine.

Frenzy! Dondrub waved a bow in one hand and a sword in the other as he twisted and reeled around the courtyard. With his face raised to the sky, he opened his mouth wide and howled.

Then he collapsed. It was sudden; he went down as if there were no body inside his cloak.

A gasp went up from the crowd. After scrutinizing the heap of colorful silk and silver, the people glanced at one another. A few snickered nervously. Dondrub's robe was so ample that his limp body could hardly be seen beneath it. They began taking a step or two toward the robe.

But then Dondrub leaped up. This time he no longer twirled wildly. Instead his movements were leaden and lumbering.

Dondrub lifted the steel mirror that hung around his neck. He gripped it in both hands and stared into it for a long time. When Dondrub eventually looked up from the mirror, his eyes were glassy and his slack cheeks trembled.

The audience pressed in closer, those in the back row butting their way toward the front. Thunder moved in near enough to see the oracle's eyes. They were flat, as if he were seeing a vision. "The iron raven roosts, its claws dripping red!" he cried in a high-pitched and unearthly singsong. "Monkey spawn is cast out—or dead. Or dead!"

Like a receding wave, the audience fell back, gasping. Dondrub's words were yet to be interpreted, but the meaning was obviously bad, and no one had expected anything bad on the day of a holy child's arrival.

After Dondrub had finished prophesying, after Thunder and Pounder had marched back into his chamber, Thunder shrugged off the dragon cloak and hurried back into the courtyard. The crowd was breaking up, and the tulku and Lama Tsab-Chang both were gone. As Thunder shuffled toward the staircase with the rest of the audience, one of the older monks motioned him over. "Son, you are the nephew of Lama Gyalo, right?"

"Yes, Kushog."

"Look." He held out a necklace of turquoise prayer beads, a different scene carved into each one. "It's the tulku's." The monk smiled, thinking of the little boy. "He was falling asleep as they carried him off, and I saw the beads drop out of his hand. Will you take them to his house?"

"Of course, Kushog."

"Good boy. Give them to our tulku himself."

"Yes, Kushog." Thunder set off down the stone stairway toward the little tulku's house. As he approached it, though, dread overcame him: Pounder, with his big key weapon at his waist, was arriving to take over guarding the wide front steps. He gazed down at Thunder without smiling.

Keeping his head bowed, Thunder began mounting the steps. Pounder's huge feet slid sideways to block his way.

Panic made Thunder light-headed as warily he looked up at the dub dub. He stepped up another stair.

"Kitchen Boy," Pounder growled, "first you refuse to work for me; then you become Dondrub's guard instead. I see what you're up to. You aspire to become captain of the dub dubs in my place."

Stiff with tension, Thunder managed to shake his head.

Pounder smirked at him. "You have become a guard because you wanted not to be a guard?"

Thunder swallowed. Courage, he commanded himself silently. He stepped up another stair. Pounder stepped down one.

Thunder whispered about the prayer beads held tight against his chest, "I have these for the tulku."

Pounder started to step down to the step one above Thunder's, then pretended to slip. He fell against Thunder, butting him down off the steps. Thunder landed hard and lay heaving. He managed to lift his head, then put out his hand to steady himself. When he opened it, his palm was dirty with blood and grit. He wobbled up onto his feet.

"Go away, Kitchen Boy."

Thunder's throat was as dry as leather. "I have to give these to the tulku," he insisted, clutching the prayer beads.

"Give them to me," Pounder said, holding out his hand.

Thunder tightened his grip on the beads. "I'm supposed to give them to the tulku."

Pounder's eyes narrowed. "Don't trust me, eh?" he asked. "Or respect me. Why not? Am I not a monk, like you?"

"Of course I trust and respect—"

"If you did, you would have come to work for me. Instead you go live with the great Lama Gyalo and even become Dondrub's guard. No, you'll work for anyone but me. I've seen your type before."

A sound came from behind; in the split second while Pounder turned to look, Thunder bolted past him. He heard Pounder's heavy feet thudding as he ran after him. But Thunder was inside the house and darting along dark hallways and up and down stairs. He rounded a corner and slipped into an alcove to hide.

Thunder stood panting in the semidarkness, pressing his back against the wall. He'd run so hard that he thought he was going to vomit. Around him the mud-walled corridors were lit by the flickering glow of butter lamps set into niches.

On the opposite wall Pounder's shadow appeared. His shape showed that he was holding up his big key weapon as if it were a club. As Pounder drew close to the aura cast by the nearest butter lamp, Thunder put both hands over his mouth to quiet his breathing. He squeezed his eyes shut. He was afraid to look, afraid the shadow would grow bigger, afraid Pounder would leap out. . . .

He heard Pounder's footsteps retreating and opened his eyes. Pounder's shadow was gone, and in his relief Thunder began to sink down against the wall. But abruptly he forced himself up. He looked down at the tulku's prayer beads. He couldn't wait to complete this task that should have been easy and was instead so difficult.

He crept along the windowless hallway, searched side rooms for the tulku, and eventually stepped outside into what he'd expected to be a courtyard. But in his mad dash from Pounder he had become lost and was not in a courtyard but on an upstairs balcony. He leaned over the half wall to see whether Pounder was below. Down there the compound was empty.

He turned around, then froze. Pounder stood behind him, gently slapping his key weapon in the palm of his hand. Looming close, he rumbled dangerously, "What do you have against me, Kitchen Boy?"

"I . . . don't have . . ."

"I suppose we were enemies in a past lifetime . . . or in many past lifetimes."

Thunder tried to run away. He jerked forward and flung his arms out to push Pounder aside. But his hand caught Pounder on the chin as if he'd slapped him.

Pounder roared with outrage. He lunged at Thunder. Thunder sprang to the left. Pounder crashed against the balcony half wall. He spun around. He lifted the key weapon and slashed it down beside Thunder's head. Thunder twisted away; the key whipped past him.

Thunder leaped into the corner. He held his hands out for protection. Pounder slammed up against him and forced him flat against the balcony half wall. Thunder tried to speak, but all that came out was a gasp. The wall's rough texture pressed into the backs of his legs, hurting him.

"Stay away from me, Kitchen Boy, and I'll stay away from you." Pounder reared back and butted Thunder hard.

Another crack, louder than the first one, split the silence. It occurred to Thunder that behind him the balcony half wall was collapsing. He used all his strength to pull himself away from the cracking wall, to safety.

But as the half wall broke, Pounder tumbled past him into the gap.

Thunder heard a loud thud from below.

He stood frozen. It took all his effort to drag himself around and make himself look down.

Pounder was down there, sprawled out and still.

16

▾ ▾ ▾

THUNDER TURNED AWAY and vomited. When he looked down into the courtyard again, he saw a second dub dub standing over Pounder and squinting up. Fear surged into Thunder's head and clouded his eyes. His vision went wavy; the dub dub seemed to float forward and back as if he were part of a dream.

As he stood dumbfounded, he realized that the dub dub was calling him, saying, "Run! Get away, Dzo."

But Thunder just stood there.

The dub dub slapped the side of his thigh. "Get away!"

The slap brought Thunder back to some kind of awareness. He nodded feebly and, still clutching the turquoise prayer beads, stumbled away.

A veil of horror enveloped him, bringing with it a feverish obsession with finding the tulku and returning his beads. It was as if never in the history of humankind had any task been so important. Sometimes staggering as the image of Pounder leaped into his mind afresh, he blundered into one empty room after another. At last he came to one where a monk sat meditating on a tiger-skin rug. The monk was utterly still except for his hands, which moved in rhythm with his quiet chanting. His chest filled out his robe like a yak driver's. His broad face was darkened by tiny wrinkles, and his blunt nose, creased down the middle, hadn't much of a bridge. On his thick neck one pulsating tendon stood out like a rope.

Thunder tottered forward toward the firelight. He stood watching the meditator for a full minute before a sob came involuntarily out of his throat.

At the sound the monk calmly laid his hands in his lap, then opened his eyes. In silence he gazed up at Thunder.

Thunder took another step forward. "I came—" He swallowed. "The tulku dropped his beads and—"

"Thank you. I am Lama Namkha, his tutor," the monk said, leaning forward to take them. "You can give them to me."

"Kushog," Thunder said, calming down a little now that he was speaking, "I was told I must give them only to the tulku himself."

"All right then," the monk said, standing up willingly, "I'll get—"

So close to completing what had become a nearly impossible task, Thunder closed his eyes and dropped his chin onto his chest. Something inside him snapped. He had come to this holy place to become a religious man, had put on this robe. And now . . . "I killed Pounder," he moaned.

Lama Namkha sat back down hard.

Thunder covered his face with his hands.

"Tell me," the monk said quietly.

Thunder's story didn't come out smoothly but full of stammers and doubt. It all seemed dreamy and untrue.

When Thunder finished, Lama Namkha stood up without commenting and left the room. Thunder waited in misery, but soon Lama Namkha returned. "I looked in the courtyard," he said. "Pounder's body is gone. Who told you to run?"

"I don't know," Thunder groaned.

"Whoever it was, he must have found a servant to help him take Pounder to the medical lama.

"Pounder—" Lama Namkha went on, shaking his head. Then, instead of finishing his sentence, he asked, "Are you even sure Pounder was dead?"

"Oh! No, I . . . But he was so still—" Thunder stopped, then asked, "What will happen to me? What should I do?"

"What will happen to any of us?" Lama Namkha murmured. "Dondrub's prophecy . . ." But then he glanced up as if he'd forgotten that Thunder was there. "We must ask," he said, and strode over to a silver chest, knelt beside it, and carefully lifted out a bundle of yellow silk. Carrying it in both hands like an offering, he took the parcel to the hearth. There he painstakingly unwrapped it. Inside lay the polished shoulder blade of a sheep. After praying, Lama Namkha placed the bone in the fire, and they sat listening to it pop and watching cracks form. When the crackling stopped, Lama Namkha removed it from the fire. He examined it in silence before saying, "The oracle bone says that Pounder is not dead."

Thunder didn't know if that was good news or bad. All he knew was that suddenly he was caught in an even worse horror than the one that had caused him to flee Chu Lungba. He bit down hard on the insides of his cheeks, then handed the tulku's beads to Lama Namkha. He didn't care anymore whether he gave them only to the tulku, as he'd been told. He was sick of obeying his elders. He blamed obedience for the series of events that had eventually forced him to abandon familiar places, abandon people who loved him, abandon all that was safe. He groaned and repeated, "What must I do?"

At first Lama Namkha didn't answer; he only gazed at Thunder. Then, "I recognize you," he said, narrowing his eyes appraisingly. "Aren't you the nephew of my friend Lama Gyalo?"

"Yes, Kushog."

"Hmm. Well, he is wise, and he is your teacher. You must ask him your questions, not me."

17

▼ ▼ ▼

THUNDER WAS ASHAMED and couldn't speak to his uncle of what had happened. He dragged himself through the rest of the day, feeling nothing but numbness and pain as he listened to the buzz of comments around him: "No one knows whether Pounder's karma . . ." "His old mother is coming to . . ." "If he dies, how will such a death affect his rebirth if . . ." The concerned tone behind each comment left Thunder with the new and uncomfortable realization that Pounder was human; he was even a son to someone.

The next morning, as Thunder stared into his cabinet, holding the doors open on either side as a way to hide his face from Zang-po, Gyalo bustled in from a meeting with some of the other important lamas.

"Nephew!" he crowed. "You have met my old friend Lama Namkha!"

Dread dropped over Thunder like a blanket. "Yes, Aku," he admitted, still hiding his face.

From behind, Gyalo laid his long hand on Thunder's shoulder. Thunder shuddered, thinking that this was the same hand that had plucked the gul-gyan from their rightful place in the gompa treasury. "Our tulku is homesick and lonely," Gyalo went on. "Can you believe it: Lama Namkha wants *you*, of all the boys here at the gompa, to be his companion."

Slowly Thunder looked over his shoulder at First Aku. "Why?"

"Why!" First Aku repeated, chuckling. "When great opportunities come our way, must we ask why?" He knelt on the floor next to Thunder. "Why? Perhaps because Lord Buddha has opened Lama Namkha's eyes to the same fine qualities I see in you." He lifted his hand, his index finger extended. "'Though the sky is filled with bright stars, who can notice them if the sun itself stands with them?'"

Looking at the floor, Thunder shook his head.

"Why look so . . . broken, Nephew, in the face of such joy?" Gyalo touched him under the chin and tipped his face upward. "You, chosen from among every boy at the gompa. What a great triumph!" First Aku glanced down at the copper canister of butter that he held in his hand and the ceremonial scarf hanging over his forearm. His voice turned grave as he added, "Did you hear the interpretation of Dondrub's prophecy, Nephew?"

"No. What—"

"Remember what the great saint Padmasambhava said hundreds of years ago? 'When the iron bird flies and horses move on wheels, Tibetans will be scattered like ants around the world.'"

"Of course. I know the prophecy as well as I know my own name. Everyone does."

First Aku nodded. "And Dondrub's strange words . . ." He closed his eyes and pressed both hands to his temples. "They mean that the time has arrived for Padmasambhava's prophecy to come true. 'Claws dripping red'—that is the red of blood, of course. 'Monkey spawn' refers to Tibetans, for our legends say that Tibetans descend from the legendary queen and the monkey."

"But what does 'cast out—or dead' mean?"

"Like Padmasambhava so long ago, Dondrub meant that Tibetans will be scattered over the earth. Or killed." Shaking his head, he added, "Hard times are coming. Hard. Hard."

"Dondrub could be wrong," Thunder said weakly.

First Aku shook his head. "He is not wrong. I have anticipated this for a long time."

"Really, Aku?"

First Aku smiled sadly. "Do not think me a great sage, Nephew. I have only seen . . . signs. Tibet is on the brink of change. My life, your life, we live not so differently from Padmasambhava a thousand years ago. But your generation will be the last to live in this unchanged way. Those younger than you . . ." He struggled for words but in the end said only, "Their lives will be different."

"How different could life ever be at Tharpa Dok?"

First Aku glanced swiftly at him but didn't answer. Instead he said, "I am going to offer butter at the Temple of the Oracle. Would you like to come pray with me and to thank Lord Buddha for your rare opportunity to know the tulku?"

Thunder had forgotten that behind them Zang-po must be listening to everything. But now the servant boy leaped forward. "*I* will come with you, Kushog," he said eagerly.

Gyalo didn't seem to hear. "Nephew?" he prompted.

Thunder shook his head. He wanted to stay away from First Aku as much as possible; he didn't want to be with his uncle when he learned about the part Thunder had played in Pounder's fall.

"Next time then." First Aku placed both hands on Thunder's shoulders and sighed proudly. "Samjam Rimpoche is many incarnations older than you. Yet in this incarnation you are older than he. As you get to know him, teach him wisely."

Thunder gazed at him blankly, wondering what, if anything, he knew worth teaching to anyone else.

Behind them Zang-po asked weakly, "Kushog—?"

First Aku glanced around and smiled at him.

"Would you like to come with me, Zang-po?"

Suddenly Zang-po looked shy and uncertain.

Thunder burst out, "Aku, yes, take Zang-po with you. I'm not free right now, but he—"

"Of course." Gyalo glanced back at Zang-po. "Come along then," he said, and swept out of the house.

Zang-po scurried to follow Gyalo, but hesitated at the door and cast a wistful glance back at Thunder. "What makes you special enough to be the tulku's friend?" he murmured.

Thunder said quietly, "Zang-po, believe me, I'm not special."

"To our tutor you're the one and only." Zang-po's shoulders sagged. He lowered his head to his chest and rolled his eyes up to look at Thunder. "Just once," he said, "I wish he would think the sun shines out of *my* backside—like in the old days, before you came."

A pang went through Thunder. "Zang-po, I wish it, too."

18

▼ ▼ ▼

THE NEXT DAY Thunder went to the tulku's house for the second time. The child had delicate features, with a pointed chin and flyaway eyebrows. Dressed in the usual burgundy robe and sucking on his lower lip, he sat beside Lama Namkha. He was gazing up at the tutor as if he were a magical talking yak.

Bashfully Thunder drew back from the doorway, then took a deep breath and stumbled into the room. When student and teacher both looked up, startled, he stuck out his tongue respectfully. "Kushog, Rimpoche," he stammered, politely addressing them both.

"Ah! This must be your new friend, Tulku-la," Lama Namkha said, putting his arm around the child's shoulder. "Can you tell him he's welcome?"

"Welcome," the little boy chirped, his mouth hanging open as he stared at Thunder with big eyes.

"Your name is—"

"Thondup Dorje, Kushog."

"Thondup Dorje," the tutor repeated. Then he went on in a gentle rumble. "This is little Lobsang-Samjam-Tsewang-Sandara-Mig-Puntsog. You may call him Samjam Rimpoche."

"I am honored, Samjam Rimpoche," Thunder said.

"Can he call me just Samjam instead of by the title Rimpoche?" the tulku asked eagerly.

"I see no harm in it."

"Because all is impermanence, and in our next lifetimes perhaps Dorje will be more important than I am?" the child added uncertainly.

"We're all important . . . but that's the idea," the tutor said, smiling at Thunder over Samjam's head. "You learned today's lesson well: impermanence in everything—even in who we are." He touched Samjam lightly on the nose. "Impermanence—hmm! Perhaps impermanence means that this time around, you will be a more diligent student than when I taught you in your last lifetime."

"Because I *am* a whole incarnation older now," the child reminded his teacher earnestly. "Kushog, how old was I when I died? Was I twenty yet?"

Lama Namkha sighed. "Let's talk of happier things than the last time you passed beyond sorrow. It was my most painful lesson in impermanence, and I have waited for nine long years to see you again. Dorje," he added, turning to Thunder, "today is unseasonably warm. You may take Tulku-la outside to walk in the courtyard." He turned back to the tulku. "Dorje will be a better friend for you than a dried weed like me."

The little boy put his hand into his tutor's. "No one could be a better friend than you, Kushog," he said.

Lama Namkha chuckled. "He's a special little fellow," he told Thunder as he rubbed Samjam's bristly hair. "But, Tulku-la, no more ideas about running away on a big adventure."

Thunder had been impatiently waiting through the chitchat to ask his question: "Am I here because Pounder—?"

Lama Namkha held up a hand to stop Thunder from finishing his sentence. "That one you speak of is vengeful, and so are a few of his warriors," he said, then glanced at Samjam, who sat placidly gazing at them as they spoke of things he couldn't understand. "In life, efforts to seek revenge are sometimes thwarted simply because the victim is friends with important people." He raised his eyebrows at Thunder, apparently reluctant to speak more clearly in front of Samjam. "You have confided in your aku, as I suggested?"

Thunder stared bleakly at the floor, and in answer Lama Namkha only sighed and shook his head.

After Lama Namkha left them at the temple steps, Thunder shook off his worries. As he sat down next to Samjam, the child asked, "Can *I* decide what to do now?"

"Anything you want."

Samjam's lip began to tremble. "Then I want you to take me home to my ama."

"Oh . . . no," Thunder said uncomfortably.

"But you said 'anything,'" Samjam said, unwilling to meet his eye.

"I can't do *that*, though. I'm sorry. Talk to your tutor about it."

Samjam was silent, fiddling with the edge of his robe. After a pause he said, "If I talk to him about it, he will feel sad. I don't want to make him sad."

Thunder put his arm around Samjam and gazed across the courtyard at one of Pounder's dub dubs. Not knowing whether talking would make Samjam feel better or worse, he asked tentatively, "Where is home?" But Samjam didn't answer, and when Thunder looked down at him, he saw big tears rolling down his cheeks. "Samjam—" he said.

But Samjam cut him off in a rush: "Home is . . . I feed the chickens all by myself, and my pony must be wondering where I am! And one day men came and they were monks and they had some things." Samjam turned and looked up at Thunder pleadingly. "Three prayer wheels and four strings of beads and a few tsampa bowls and things like that, and they asked me which prayer wheel I liked best and which beads and which—and which—and that if I picked well, I could keep the things I chose for the rest of my life." He closed both hands on a fold of his robe and stared down at it. "And

I *did* pick well. Every single thing I picked was something that had belonged to the tulku of Tharpa Dok, who had died, and so they said I am him in his next incarnation, and at first I didn't understand, but they gave me his name anyway and I will never be called Little Radish anymore."

Thunder smiled. "Hello, Little Radish." He knew all about the choosing ritual that determined whether a child would be named as a tulku. But he could imagine how confusing it must have been to a boy as young as Samjam.

Samjam buried his face in Thunder's side. When he came up for air, he said, "They didn't say that choosing well would mean leaving my ama. I thought my ama would tell them, 'No! No! You cannot have my Little Radish!' But I have a baby sister who is always sick, and my ama told me that I was lucky to come here, and I must pray for her and be her very own tulku and that my being a tulku is the only thing that can keep her alive." He heaved a big gulp.

"I miss my ama, too," Thunder murmured, gazing down at Samjam's narrow shoulders.

The child put out his chin. "I'm finished crying now." Another gulp came out of him, and he held his breath to stop any more of them. After a long pause he let out his breath. "There! And I'm not going to cry anymore—I'm the tulku." He cocked his head to examine Thunder from a different angle. "I'm wondering who I should have you be."

"What do you mean?"

"Do you know," Samjam said, screwing up his face with the effort of explaining, "how when you first meet someone, it's easier to talk to him if you pretend that he's someone you already know? Your brother, for example, or your friend. Once you're well acquainted, you can stop pretending."

Thunder leaned away from him, surprised to hear a child say such a strange thing, with his expression so grave.

"I'll pretend you're my big cousin Penlop." Samjam rubbed his forearm across his face, and his last tears were gone.

"All right . . . and I would pretend you're my brother Joker, but I can already see that you're not like him at all."

Samjam looked worried. "Is there no one like me?"

"No one. But that's all right. I want to pretend that you're you."

"Then you don't need to pretend at all," Samjam said, grinning, "because I *am* me."

They soon tired of the courtyard, and Thunder lifted Samjam up onto his shoulders so that he could look over the high wall. Then he led Samjam behind his house toward the horses. A cold breeze puffed up the dust as they ran to the stables, where they made faces and wiped their sleeves over their tongues to clear the dust out of their mouths.

The stables were surprisingly warm after the cold

and windy courtyard. Thunder showed the tulku how to dig tunnels in the straw, creating caves for them to wiggle into together.

"I know a good place for walking, Samjam," Thunder said as the boy sat braiding bits of straw. "When it's warmer, we'll go there and I'll find twigs and stones and make you a game."

Samjam began wriggling out of the straw cave. "A game will feel just like being home." He looked up at Thunder seriously. "There are no games at Tharpa Dok," he said, shaking his head hard. "Study. Meditate. Pray." On each word Samjam bumped his small fist down on the ground. Then he opened his hand and looked at his empty palm. "No games."

"Not yet, but that's why Lama Namkha asked me to come to you. It will be all right."

With Lama Namkha's reluctant approval and two dub dubs strolling behind, they walked down to the stream where, as a kitchen boy, Thunder had cleaned the big copper kettles.

They combed the stream bank for a *dibshing*, a special twig said to make one invisible. As Thunder stood examining an odd-looking twig, he said, "Look, Samjam. This one might—" He glanced around. "Samjam? Samjam!" He flung down the twig and began running, but before he got far, Samjam came sauntering toward him. "Samjam! Where were you?"

Samjam gazed at him blankly. "Over there."

"Don't go off like that again!"

"No? Why not?" Samjam asked mildly.

Thunder flung up his hands. "Because I'm here to protect you!"

"*You*? Protect *me*? I didn't know!"

Thunder looked away; he found it uncomfortable to meet Samjam's eyes.

"Excuse me, Dorje," Samjam said, lightly touching the older boy's arm. "I see what you thought. Your body is larger than mine, so you presumed . . ." His voice fell away; his smile was so gentle that all Thunder's worry disappeared. But Thunder had the sudden and uncomfortable feeling that by initiating the dibshing search, he was not entertaining Samjam as much as Samjam was humoring him. "Come on, then," Thunder mumbled, not knowing how to handle the little tulku except to go on with the game. "But if I'm to call you Samjam, you call me Thunder."

"All right, Thunder."

"So. We must toss any twig we find into the river to see if it sails upstream and not down," Thunder said. "According to legend, such a stick must be a dibshing."

"But if it does go upriver, it will be gone," Samjam reasoned, hugging himself tightly against the wind.

"Then we would leap into the river and snatch it back."

Samjam said calmly, "But I would drown. I can't swim, you see."

Thunder laughed. "But you would be holding on to the dibshing, and it would make you invisible! Does drowning matter if you drown invisibly?" When Samjam's face stayed serious, Thunder prompted, "Just a joke, small brother."

None of the twigs they found made them invisible. Flinging the last one away, Thunder said, "Next time we'll look for spirits instead. You can see them, they say, if you rub magpies' blood across your eyes."

Samjam put his hand on Thunder's arm. "But I wouldn't like to kill a bird," he said earnestly. "Lama Namkha says that loving-kindness should extend even to demons. So doesn't that mean we must surely protect innocent animals?"

Thunder chuckled. "You know, I hadn't thought of it that way. I wouldn't like to kill a magpie myself."

19

▼ ▼ ▼

WHEN THUNDER ARRIVED home that night, he remembered with dread that he still hadn't confided in his uncle. He sat on the khang, stared blankly at a wide wooden page of scripture, and struggled for the courage to talk to First Aku.

But he couldn't concentrate; two days had passed since he'd nearly killed Pounder, and no one but Lama Namkha—and the dub dub who'd told Thunder to run—seemed even to know Thunder had had any part in the accident. And why had that dub dub told him to run? Maybe he thinks I pushed Pounder, Thunder thought. I didn't push him, did I? The more he tried to remember, the more uncertain he became.

Apparently the dub dub was keeping silent about

Thunder's secret, but would he stay silent forever?

Thunder realized that First Aku was standing before him and looked up. "What did you say?" he asked vacantly.

"I said, never have I seen you this absorbed in your studies," First Aku said warmly. "You shall yet become a scholar and in manhood will be all I ever hoped." With shining eyes he sighed and turned away.

Thunder stared at his uncle's back. Absorbed in his studies . . . all he ever hoped . . . With a sense of horror, he held his hands out before him. Once it had mattered that they were big, hard hands able to labor until they bled. They were still big. But all the calluses he'd earned with his pain and sweat were peeling or gone. His hands were going soft.

As if he'd read his nephew's thoughts, Gyalo turned from where he stood adjusting the small water bowls on the altar. "What did you say?" he asked Thunder brightly.

"I . . ." Thunder dropped his hands in his lap and stared down at the page of script. Now was his chance to confess about Pounder. But he was afraid. Besides, now that he knew about the gul-gyan, his heart was closed to his uncle. "I said nothing," he said softly.

After his uncle had gone, Thunder set aside the wooden page on which he could read only a few of the simplest words. Although the evening was still young, and he would be missed from prayer assembly, he lay down to sleep and, for a little while, to forget.

During the first few weeks after the tulku arrived, the gompa was charged with excitement. Even the most taciturn monks chattered about their favorite topic, the little boy. But once Samjam was settled, the gompa fell back into its normal routine. Now the ordinary monks glimpsed the tulku only as he glided past the windows of his house or when he took the few steps from his doorway to a closed palanquin and was whisked away.

Whenever Thunder led Samjam through the gompa, the pilgrims clustered around them, their faces shining in awe. Thunder would step back and let the child be the center of attention. But for the pilgrims, seeing the tulku was never enough. Speaking to him was better; touching him was fantastic. "When my hand brushed against his robe," one of them told Thunder, "I felt Nirvana through my fingertips."

But when Samjam's distressed eyes turned to Thunder, the older boy would touch the younger protectively on his shoulder. At that Samjam's admirers would glide away wide-eyed as if instead of offering them words, the tulku had placed rubies in their outstretched, begging hands.

Thunder spent time with Samjam as often as he could. He made the child toys: slingshots, crude dice, and a bow and arrow.

"Ping!" Samjam cried, releasing the arrow. "Thunder, can we go on an adventure and shoot arrows a long, long way? Please?"

"Outside the gompa? Oh, I don't think so."

"But Thunder—"

"No more of that. Now, Samjam, see if you can aim well enough to hit that stump."

When Thunder arrived home that day, First Aku was pacing back and forth from the altar to the kitchen door. Thunder made a sound, and First Aku spun around, his face a mask of agony. "You never told me." He was wringing his hands.

Thunder had never seen him like this and stood gawking, still holding the door open behind him. "What is it, Aku?" he asked, though dread rose in his throat; First Aku must know that he'd been with Pounder when he fell.

Gyalo spun away from him, breathing hard. Then he turned back. "How could you do such a thing, and how could you keep it secret from me? 'Even if a snake has a gem in its mouth, never hold it near your heart!'"

"What are you saying? Am *I* that snake?"

"You—" First Aku flashed at him. Then, instead of finishing, he whirled away from Thunder, stalked over to the altar, and leaned against it.

Thunder was filled with confusion and guilt. He wanted to say, "It was an accident," but First Aku's back looked so rigid and unyielding. . . .

Without turning, First Aku began, "Nephew, I thought I understood your character. I would have thought you'd face up to what you've done to Pounder, and accept—"

"First Aku," Thunder heard himself saying, "you don't understand."

Like a stampeding horse, Gyalo went on with his own speech. "And accept your responsibility to make amends. Why did you not tell me? Why?"

Cold horror crept up Thunder's spine.

First Aku punched one hand into the other, then started pacing again. "'Though a man has neither fur coat nor paws, if he has fangs, then he is a beast!'"

Stunned, Thunder cried out, "Do you think I *tried* to kill him?"

First Aku stopped pacing. With his chest heaving, he stared at Thunder.

"You *do* think it! It was nothing like that!"

First Aku closed his eyes. He drew a deep breath, then asked softly, "Do you find me so simple? The finish of that soul's one meager incarnation as Pounder is hardly important—not in light of his thousands of incarnations. But have you learned nothing of what I've taught you?"

Thunder looked away in confusion and wiped his sweaty hands on the sides of his robe.

First Aku raised a forefinger to signal that another quotation was coming: "'Having never been anything but a goldfish, the goldfish cannot know what it means to be a goldfish.' A person like Pounder can never change unless a very different being shows him the way. The issue is not whether Pounder lives or dies," First Aku went on, "nor exactly how karma assigned you a hand in his fate. What matters is that you have had *any* input into it. Your karma and Pounder's are now entwined indefinitely. Unless in this lifetime you pay off your karma to him, you and he will still be tethered together in your next lifetime and in the next and the next."

"I don't care," Thunder moaned, squeezing his hands into fists.

"Of course you care. By affecting Pounder's destiny in this significant way, you have bound yourself to him more absolutely than if your bodies were lashed together with ropes." He searched Thunder's face, and the boy stared back at him in shock. "Instead of allowing yourself to stay shackled to him, you must transform his spirit, thereby freeing him from his base nature and freeing yourself from him." After a long silence First Aku finished like a death knell. "So now you understand."

What if First Aku was right? Feeling as if his mouth were full of uncombed wool and his heart carved from granite, Thunder managed to ask, "What exactly would you have me do?"

Aku smacked his hand down on Thunder's cupboard. "You must mentor Pounder as I have mentored you. Conversation, guidance, loving-kindness."

Thunder stared in dead numbness at the floor. Then without lifting his head, he rolled his eyes up to look at his uncle. He felt the same cold fear that had crept into him when Ama said, "You must leave Chu Lungba," when Second Aku said, "You must live in the kitchen," when Seventh Hand said, "You must not be my friend. You were never Dzo."

"Must." Always "must." Anything else "was not the way." But he couldn't believe that his mentor, his defender was—just like everyone else—telling him "must." First Aku, whom once he had honored above Apa, trusted above Ama, loved above Lord Buddha himself. First Aku. There had been a time when First Aku had asked nothing more of Thunder than to listen.

But now this.

"*Must,*" Thunder said out loud from the spreading coldness deep, deep in his heart.

"'Must,'" First Aku echoed, his expression changing from panic to relief. Clearly he didn't hear the change in Thunder's tone, didn't see that his nephew was frozen against him, didn't even suspect that deep inside Thunder's sunny nature there could be a remote place that was as frozen as snow.

"You must become Pounder's beacon," First Aku said eagerly, "as I have been yours. And you must start at once because he was paralyzed in the fall and could go beyond sorrow anytime. So. You must move him beyond the narrow man he has been to the monk filled with loving-kindness that he can become. To do such a great deed for him will surely pay off the karma you owe him."

There was a long silence, during which First Aku's expression became less confident.

"So," Thunder said hollowly. "That is what I *must* do."

"Yes. Then you do understand." First Aku pulled Thunder to him. With his hands on Thunder's shoulders, he moved him to arm's length to get a good look at him. "Thank you, Lord Buddha," he whispered, his eyes closed.

Thunder pulled away stiffly. "Samjam must be waiting for me," he mumbled, unable to meet First Aku's eyes.

"Yes, go to him now. But tomorrow—"

Thunder turned and started out.

"Nephew?" First Aku called after him. "You understand why I spoke so strongly to you? You grasp the significance of Pounder's karma, aside from how he acts in this petty lifetime?"

Thunder glanced around and saw his uncle's head cocked questioningly. "Of course, Aku," he said smoothly. But that cold place inside him hadn't dissolved.

20

▼ ▼ ▼

THUNDER STRODE INTO the room where Samjam sat waiting and slid onto the khang next to him. Samjam looked up at Thunder with his lower lip stuck out. "You're late," he accused. "Now we won't have any chance to play before prayer assembly." He crossed his arms over his chest. "And I even have a present for you," he said.

"You do?"

Frowning, Samjam pointed to a ceremonial hat, gold-embroidered with a medallion in front, that lay farther down on the khang.

"What's this?"

"Look underneath."

Thunder plucked up the hat, but there was nothing

inside. Samjam scrambled up onto his knees to look over Thunder at the place on the khang where the hat had been. "It's gone!"

"What was it?"

"I caught a sunbeam in the hat." He turned to point toward the spot in front of the window where the light fell on the floor. "There it is again!" he said, amazed. "That's right where I caught it."

"Samjam, the light is from outside. It comes in through the window, but only a little ways. It always stays right there in that spot."

Samjam scowled harder. "Just like me. I stay right *here*," he said, smacking his hand on his knee.

Thunder was silent for a long time, imagining one thing or another he could say. He didn't think about the consequences that any of his words might have. He was too filled with defiance to think through anything right now. The words that finally sprang out of his mouth surprised him as much as they did Samjam: "If you're sure you want an adventure, I'll take you out."

Samjam searched his face, astounded. "Out of Tharpa Dok? Would leaving Tharpa Dok be my adventure?"

"Call it what you like. *I* want to get out, too."

"Are you teasing me?" Samjam asked, his eyes big. He slipped off the khang, ran to the window, and pushed open the shutters, then spun around. "An adventure outside the gompa walls?"

In spite of the turmoil inside him, Thunder smiled.

It was hard to keep the cold place quite so cold when he looked into the tulku's small, warm face. He nodded. "Outside the walls."

Samjam leaped to his feet. "Right now!"

Thunder knitted his brows, thinking hard. He felt rebellious to his fingertips; it would serve them right if he took their tulku away. And why not now? He slapped both hands down on his thighs. "Right now," he agreed.

But then the drone of the conch floated over the gompa. "Oh, no," Samjam groaned. "Listen, it's already time for prayer assembly. We can't go."

From the hallway Thunder heard footsteps. "Hush!" He gripped Samjam by the arm. "I have an idea! Did you have *momos* at breakfast?" he asked.

"Yes, but what does that—"

Lama Namkha came in, holding a hand out to them. "Prayer assembly, Tulku-la, Thunder."

Thunder bowed his head respectfully. "Kushog, Samjam's stomach is aching. He says he ate too many momos this morning!"

"Did he? The little piglet!" said Lama Namkha, teasingly shaking a finger at Samjam.

"He asks if he can skip prayer assembly today. I'll stay with him."

"Why, thank you, Thunder. Lie down then, little one," Lama Namkha said, settling Samjam on the khang and smoothing a sheepskin over him. "But never again so many momos at once!"

"Yes, Kushog," Samjam said too happily, but Lama Namkha didn't seem to notice.

Then Lama Namkha was gone. "Stay here," Thunder told Samjam urgently, "and if anyone comes, act sick. I'll be back for you soon, and we'll go!"

Peeking around each corner first, Thunder ran through the gompa, empty because all the monks were at the prayer assembly. Surely, he realized as he ran, if they were going adventuring, he must take something of value, something with which to buy food.

At First Aku's house he went straight to the brick that hid the gul-gyan and, with his blood pounding, yanked out the metal box. He put one necklace after another into the pocket of his robe.

But after removing the fifth necklace, he sat back on his haunches and stared down at the string of beads draped over his hands. This fifth gul-gyan was the very same necklace Zang-po had used to stroke his cheek when he had shown Thunder First Aku's stash. Confusion washed over Thunder; he put both hands to his head and groaned.

Never in his life had he felt so bewildered. Where would he take Samjam? What would they do there? Would they ever return? One by one he lay four of the necklaces back in the box and stared down at the fifth. On the other hand, what had First Aku ever done for him that he couldn't take just one? It had seemed as if First Aku were helping him; that much was true. But all the time perhaps he'd been manipulating him instead. . . .

He slipped the fifth gul-gyan into the pocket of his chuba, pushed the metal box back into the recess, replaced the brick, and brushed the silt from the floor.

When Thunder reached him, Samjam still lay on the khang as Thunder had directed. But instead of feigning sickness, he was thrashing around happily and singing a farmyard song to himself. Thunder scolded him with a smile. Then, to avoid the dub dub guarding the front steps, he hoisted Samjam up and out a side window and slipped out after him.

"But how will we get out of the gompa?" Samjam asked, pulling on Thunder's robe as he peeked around a corner to make sure the paths were empty of monks.

Thunder glanced around. "Wait and see," he said, reaching for the child's hand. He led Samjam up paths that the tulku had never walked before.

"When will the adventure part start?" Samjam asked, skipping along at Thunder's side.

"Guess what? It has started already because now we're on our way to the one place in the gompa that is more different from your house than any other spot within these walls. Look." Thunder pushed open the big kitchen doors. His former home was just as he'd left it. Little bowls were set out on the boards lying across each copper cauldron. There were ladders and tea cans, churns, piled yak meat, and leather bags dangling from hooks. The breeze carried the scent of simmering soup one moment and garbage the next. The smells waved over him, but where they had once made him nauseated, now they brought welcome memories. "All we need are disguises so we can sneak out of Tharpa Dok, and our disguises are right here. Can you find them?"

Samjam looked around at the heap of yak meat on the big table, the knives and skewers, the dung fuel piled near the ovens, the brooms leaning on one wall. He shook his head. In response Thunder hurried to the corner where several big cauldrons were set up on their sides, ready for any dub dubs who might come to use the tubs' grease. He gently tapped on one, and the sound reverberated like the deep and quiet tolling of a bell.

"These," he said, "are—" Thunder heard a scraping sound from near the door and spun around. He was horrified that they might be caught. By Lama Thangspa? By Norbu?

There, silhouetted in the light streaming in through the doorway, stood Seventh Hand. As the quiet bon-n-n-n-g of the cauldron still floated in the air, Samjam inched closer to Thunder and slipped his hand into the bigger boy's.

"Have you eaten, Seventh Hand?" Thunder greeted the kitchen boy cautiously.

"I have eaten," Seventh Hand murmured to Thunder, but he was staring at Samjam with round, frozen eyes.

Thunder waited, curious what name his old friend would call him by. But instead of speaking any name,

Seventh Hand bowed to Samjam, his hands in praying position. "Rimpoche, you shouldn't be in an unimportant place like this kitchen."

Thunder snorted a laugh. "Unimportant, Seventh Hand? Any monk born with a stomach would say this is the most important place in Tharpa Dok."

A flush of embarrassment crept up Seventh Hand's neck and crawled over his face. Too shy to go on looking at either Thunder or Samjam, he began picking at a loose sliver of wood on the doorjamb. "I just meant . . . I just meant . . ."

"I know. You meant 'What is he—what are they both doing here?' Seventh Hand, we're here because—" Thunder said, then fell silent.

Seventh Hand glanced up sharply. "Do you think you can't trust me?"

Thunder shifted uncomfortably and didn't answer.

Ever so slightly Seventh Hand raised his chin. "So you doubt me! Then listen to this: Tashi came straight to me."

"Tashi?"

"My brother, the dub dub. You've met him, I think. At the tulku's house."

"Do you mean it was your brother who—" Thunder dug his fingernails into his hands. To avoid looking at Seventh Hand, he busily ran his finger along the edge of the cauldron.

"Yes, the dub dub who told you to run after you

pushed Pounder off the balcony. He came straight to me and asked me whether I thought he should tell anyone what happened."

Samjam looked from one boy to the other. "What does he mean, Thunder?" he asked in a small voice.

Thunder squeezed Samjam's hand. "Seventh Hand, I didn't push him."

There was a charged pause; then Seventh Hand flung back his head dramatically. "I believe you," he said. "But even if I didn't, I wouldn't let Tashi turn you in."

Thunder crossed his arms and clamped his hands in his armpits. He gazed at Seventh Hand and thought about trust, then dropped his hands to his sides and admitted, "I'm taking Samjam on an adventure." He narrowed his eyes. "They can't stop me."

Seventh Hand stared down at the splinter of wood he'd pulled out of the doorjamb. "An adventure to do what?"

"Just an adventure," Thunder said weakly. "We'll find what we find."

Seventh Hand looked up. From the expression on his face, Thunder knew he didn't need to ask if this time, too, Seventh Hand would keep his secret.

The kitchen boy leaned against the door, and it creaked softly. "How can you get him out of Tharpa Dok?" he asked, eyeing Samjam, and Thunder gestured toward the big cauldrons. Seventh Hand looked puzzled for a moment. Then a look of understanding spread over his face. He reached behind and pulled a bag of chura off the big kitchen table. "Can I go with you, Thunder?"

"On our adventure?"

As on the night they'd met, Seventh Hand held the chura out to Thunder. But this time he was looking down shyly. "I'd like . . . another chance."

"Chance! You need no chances with me, Seventh Hand," Thunder said, digging into the bag greedily. "But hurry—and bring that chura!"

Thunder and Seventh Hand each hoisted a big cauldron onto their backs, just as they'd done whenever they took them down to the stream to clean them. Anyone watching them trudge down the slope would have needed to look closely to see that beneath the second cauldron there were two pairs of legs.

21

▼ ▼ ▼

HERE WHERE THE sky was enormous and the gritty landscape rolled out all the way to the horizon, the stone walls and prayer wheels of Tharpa Dok seemed to have vanished forever. Thunder's head knew the gompa was back there over his shoulder and that Pounder was there, too. But his heart felt utterly free of the prayers and the discipline, meditation, and calm.

After an uneasy time, during which Seventh Hand kept a respectful distance from the tulku, it seemed to strike him that Samjam was not so different from other small boys. Then the three of them knelt side by side and wove twigs and grass into odd configurations said to trap evil spirits. Thunder let Samjam do things he shouldn't: climb trees and slide down hills, even wade in the icy pool under the waterfall. Samjam lifted his robe to his knees and scampered over the flat stones, splashing as much water up on himself as if he'd let his robe hang. "Just like at home!" he whooped. "Call me Little Radish!"

At last they lay wet and muddy and exhausted and stared up at the sky. "Where's that chura?" Thunder asked, holding his hand out for the bag.

"Gone," Seventh Hand said sleepily. "We're tough adventurers, huh? No more food means time to go back."

Samjam leaped to his feet. "I'm not hungry, and I *won't* go back. I want to have more adventures!"

Thunder gawked at the little tulku, standing over them imperiously, his hands on his hips. The magnitude of stealing the tulku struck him: Samjam didn't want to go back! Horrifying! Yet Thunder dreaded going back, too. Facing First Aku, the whole community of monks, was almost too intimidating to imagine.

So he traded an indulgent smile with Seventh Hand. Then, pushed by the cold wind at their backs, they started up a long and seldom-used trail until in the distance they could see some nomads' black yak-hair tents with guns and harnesses hanging on poles, and yaks and goats milling around. A line of children, holding hands, ran kicking their heels up behind.

"We've come a long way now," Samjam said happily.

Thunder gazed at him and recalled how the monks of Tharpa Dok had stood in awe of the young boy on the day he'd arrived. How had they faced today's loss? Poor Lama Namkha must have run to First Aku's house, panicking while Gyalo assured his friend that his perfect nephew would never lead the darling of the gompa into danger.

Thunder looked around at the vast landscape, the sweeping plain and the valley to the south. Only mildly curious, he noticed a band of six or seven men working down there. Then something else struck him: The men were foreign soldiers. He knew it by their coats that were so different from chubas, the scarves tied around each man's neck, and their green goggles. Each soldier carried a "fire arrow," a rifle, slung over his shoulder. One man was looking through a tube mounted on top of a tripod. Another took measured paces away from a mark on the ground, stretching a chain out behind him as he strode. Others talked nearby. Thunder stared, outraged. Why were they measuring? Making maps?

A cloud of dust attracted his attention. First he didn't grasp what it meant. Then he groped behind him to grab the tulku. "Seventh Hand!" Thunder whispered in a choked voice. "Look!" Thirty or more Tibetans on horseback were thundering down on the foreigners, shrieking, "Ki-hu-hu-hu! Ki-hu-hu-hu!" They attacked, slicing clubs through the air and shooting matchlock muskets that had antelope horns folded under the muzzles. One threw a spear on a cord that he hauled back after each strike.

The foreigners' horses reared and broke away in

terror. The foreigners brought their fire arrows down off their shoulders and struggled to use them. But they had no chance. Against thirty Tibetans on stampeding horses, they were too few.

The boys watched in stunned horror. When Thunder felt a pulling on his sleeve, he couldn't compel himself even to look around. Foreigners. Foreigners with strange tubes and chains . . . and with guns.

All the rumors about foreigners must be true. The prophecies—Padmasambhava's, Dondrub's—must be true, too. All those warnings he'd scoffed at in Chu Lungba, all he'd ever been taught to fear—it was all true. Strangers had dared come to their homeland to measure their ground, to tear their land out from under their feet, to slaughter them.

But now the Tibetans were slaughtering them first.

"Thunder!" Seventh Hand cried, and Thunder realized the kitchen boy had been pulling on his sleeve and shouting at him for some time. "Thunder, look." Thunder blinked to pull himself out of his stupor. Samjam was walking toward the melee, holding one hand up, calling out shrilly, "Stop the killing! Lord Buddha is watching!"

Thunder ran. "Come back!" he bellowed at Samjam. But the tulku blundered on. He seemed not to see the bullets flying up ahead, seemed not to hear the shots or Thunder's call. He kept on going until Thunder reached him, saw that his eyes were unfocused as if he were in a trance, and swept him up in his arms. Clumsily

Thunder ran back with Samjam. When they were safe, he and Seventh Hand both shook the tulku by the shoulders. "Can you see us, Samjam? Samjam!"

Still strangely calm, Samjam blinked at Thunder. Hugging Samjam hard, Thunder babbled: "Samjam! I thought—Oh, Little Radish. Why did you do that? Why did you run out there?"

"They're killing," Samjam murmured.

Thunder held him close. "But you can't stop them."

Samjam pulled away, an extraordinarily distant expression on his face. There was something lordly about him as he said in a tone heavy with dignity, "I am the tulku. I thought I could make a difference."

They sat in despairing silence, Thunder with his hand on Samjam's shoulder. This time the strangers were being massacred, but surely they'd prefer to do the massacring themselves. Sorrow welled up in Thunder. "If fringies ever hurt you, Samjam," he blurted, "I will murder them myself." He clamped shut his fists. "I swear I will find a way."

Samjam jerked up as if he'd been burned. "How can you say this to me?" he demanded. "I tell you again, I am the tulku! My life is supposed to be about loving-kindness, and . . . and don't ever murder for me. Can't you guess what it feels like to be me?"

Being railed at by a five-year-old—one more elo-quent than he himself—struck Thunder dumb. They watched the battle in dejected silence until, once again childlike, Samjam buried his face in his knees. "Why are they killing?" he asked miserably. "Don't they know about loving-kindness?"

"They know," Thunder said, "but"—he floundered for words—"they forgot."

"They're dressed so strangely," Seventh Hand said. Then his mouth fell open. "They're not—?" He turned and stared at Thunder.

Thunder watched the Tibetans climbing down off their horses, kicking at the corpses, leaning down to rob them of their clothing. As the Tibetans covered their own bodies with the soldiers' coats, belts, boots, and shirts, they began to look foreign themselves.

At that moment Thunder heard a twig break behind them. Turning, he saw a foreign soldier looking at them through the sight of his fire arrow. With his goggles up on his forehead, he looked like a four-eyed insect. Instinctively all three boys stuck out their tongues respectfully. At that the soldier lowered his fire arrow slightly. He glanced at the battlefield and twisted his mouth bitterly.

Thunder began sliding toward Samjam. They were only three young monks; maybe the soldier would let them walk away.

But as he inched left, the soldier narrowed his eyes and snarled foreign words at them. Then he jabbed his fire arrow at Thunder.

"Samjam," Thunder murmured, holding his hand out to him.

The foreigner pushed the fire arrow against

Thunder's chest, jerked his chin toward where the soldiers lay dead, then growled in his own language. Thunder couldn't understand his words, but his furious, hating tone was clear.

The soldier gestured for them to walk, and they trudged along for more than an hour. Seventh Hand's limp worsened as he tired, and Samjam tottered now and then in his exhaustion. But neither boy complained.

Eventually they turned onto a narrow path that deteriorated as it twisted up an incline. At the top of the bluff a crumbling fortress stood against the evening sky. It was a flat-roofed, sprawling mass of mud and stone with thick and inward-sloping walls shot through with loopholes but no windows. The ruined walls scattered off into rubble and scrubby weeds. A number of fire arrows stood in a rack against one wall, along with neatly stacked bags and a pile of greasy rags.

Safely inside the stronghold, the soldier finally stopped prodding Thunder with the end of his fire arrow. Instead he slung it over his shoulder and shoved the boys ahead of him into a courtyard where several more soldiers lounged around. One held up a lantern to get a better look at the three young monks. So many foreigners together; the boys were outnumbered, and fear squeezed Thunder's heart.

The soldier grabbed Thunder's left ear and Seventh Hand's right and dragged them deeper into the fort. Behind, Samjam held on to a fold of Thunder's robe and scurried to keep up.

The soldier thrust them into a room that flickered golden from butter lamps. A makeshift desk, knocked together from two broken cabinets, stood to one side. Behind it an older soldier sat reading papers. He had a nearly bald head but a beard much fuller than most Tibetans could grow.

Just inside the door the soldier pulled harder on their ears, and Seventh Hand yelped. The older soldier glanced up, startled, then leaped to his feet and strode over to them. He slapped the soldier's hands away from the boys' heads and, speaking in the foreign tongue, barked at the younger man. In response the soldier lifted his hand and momentarily pressed his fingers horizontally against his forehead. After casting a disgruntled look at Thunder, he sauntered out.

Reluctantly Thunder and his companions turned to the older soldier. Unbelievably, here were the weird sky-eyes Thunder had heard about. He couldn't stop gaping at them, so much like blue glass. Were colors different, seen through such things?

The soldier stood looking at them, his hands on his hips. First his expression was cross. Then he stepped right up to Seventh Hand, who staggered back, alarmed. The man jerked back, too; he was as startled by Seventh Hand's reaction as Seventh Hand was by his approach. Questioningly the man cocked his head at Seventh Hand. Then as gently as a mother, he examined Seventh Hand's ear. "He . . . hurt you?" the man asked in accented, halting Tibetan. But when Seventh Hand only looked at his feet in shy silence, the man patted him on the shoulder, turned to Thunder, and looked at his ear, too.

Thunder reached back and pushed Samjam farther behind him. But the soldier leaned forward and held out his hand to Samjam until, sucking on his lip, the tulku shuffled out from behind Thunder and slipped his hand into the bigger boy's.

The soldier squatted and smiled at Samjam. Then, straightening up, he asked in Tibetan: "You boys . . . who?"

Thunder and Seventh Hand exchanged uncertain glances. Then Seventh Hand swept his hand down toward his burgundy robe. "You can see that we're monks."

The soldier nodded, then went striding out of the room, speaking his language to them over his shoulder as he went.

As soon as he'd gone and slammed the door after him, Samjam asked doubtfully, "Was this supposed to be part of the adventure?" He threw his arms around Thunder. "This isn't my adventure at all! I've found someone else's adventure by mistake, and where's mine? I want to go home!" he sobbed. "Mostly to my ama but—but even to Tharpa Dok!" He looked up with big eyes. "What *is* he?"

"He's a fringie."

Samjam gasped and buried his face in Thunder's stomach. Seventh Hand suddenly gripped Thunder's arm hard. "Thunder—"

Seventh Hand didn't need to finish his thought; Thunder felt he could read his friend's mind. He nodded, then spun around and tore open the door to escape. But a soldier stood guard out there, his fire arrow slung over his shoulder. Thunder hesitated, and in that instant Seventh Hand butted the guard with his shoulder and tried to push past.

But the soldier grabbed him and lightly, easily tossed him back inside. Thunder stood by, grim and silent, as the soldier sank both hands onto Samjam's shoulders and thrust him back inside with Seventh Hand. Then, with narrowed eyes, he cocked his fire arrow and stared a challenge at Thunder. It was no use, and Thunder knew it. But . . . Thunder reached into the pocket of his chuba and pulled out the gul-gyan. "Let us by," he said evenly, "and I'll give you this."

The soldier yanked the necklace out of Thunder's hand, then pushed him back inside. This time, after the door was slammed, the lock shot into the bolt.

Thunder stared in astonishment at his empty hand. Furiously he kicked the door, then fell back against the wall with his hands over his face.

22

▼ ▼ ▼

THUNDER DIDN'T KNOW how long they were left alone. He sat on the floor, and Samjam cried in his lap, fell asleep, then awoke and crawled away from the bigger boys as if he were a baby. He looked over one foreign object after another—metal tubes with glass ends, curious knives and firearms, and even a smooth, stretchy cloth. Thunder watched him despondently.

Later the older soldier came back in with yet another soldier by his side. As the door opened, the butter lamps guttered in the sudden draft. Waving a finger in Thunder's direction, the older man said a few foreign words. Then the second one said in clear Tibetan: "The colonel asks who killed his soldiers."

Thunder and Seventh Hand sat silent and resentful, Thunder with one hand on Samjam's back as he slept. The hostile atmosphere deepened before the younger man announced, "I am his translator. He speaks Tibetan, but perhaps I speak it a bit more clearly." When this statement was met with more angry stares, he barked, "If you intend to protect those savages who killed our friends, you are fools. Sooner or later you will answer my questions."

The colonel touched the man's arm and spoke to him in the foreign tongue. Then the translator said with a sigh, "He is not accusing you of joining in the rebellion yourselves. He knows that you were robbing the bodies, but—"

Samjam sat up sharply from what Thunder had thought was sleep. "We were not!" he cried, his face furious in the half-light. "We don't do such things. We're monks, and I am—"

Thunder swung around to him, flashing a "Don't tell!" warning with his eyes.

The colonel slapped his hand down on his desk. The smack silenced everyone yet again.

"Very well," the translator said, restraining his anger. "I will tell the colonel that you claim you weren't stealing." He turned and spoke to the older soldier in his own language.

The colonel waved the translator aside and stepped closer to the boys. Peering at Thunder, he said, "I . . .

perhaps you . . . not believe me. But . . . truth is . . . can trust me."

At Thunder's side, Seventh Hand snorted disbelievingly. But Thunder only passed a hand over his eyes. Why couldn't these unwelcome strangers let the three of them eat and sleep? That was all they wanted or needed just now.

The translator growled again, "Who were they?"

Then Seventh Hand surprised Thunder. He said calmly, "Each one was a Tibetan defending his own country. Any Tibetan. Every Tibetan. Not us, but—*us.*"

Thunder tried to mask his astonishment. Yet he couldn't help smiling at his friend. Seventh Hand had a way of coming through in a pinch.

"What does it matter who they were?" Seventh Hand added angrily. "You strangers have crashed your way into our country to destroy us, and they wanted to stop you. That's all."

Thunder surprised himself by adding simply, "You and your warriors are not wanted here."

The translator scowled deeply and spoke to the older soldier, who looked utterly weary as he muttered his answer in the foreign tongue. "You're lucky boys," the translator said, stepping up next to him again. "The colonel commands only that you promise never again to steal from British soldiers . . . living or dead."

British soldiers—Ingi-li. The word was an icicle down Thunder's neck. He saw from the colonel's pained face that he wanted the boys not to mind that the

Ingi-li were there; he wanted not to be hated. Thunder remembered how earlier he had made his soldier stop pulling them by their ears. Perhaps this one foreign man, if only this one, was not monstrous, as Tibetans presumed. There was also the foreigner Thunder had met near Chu Lungba—that was two.

"We're monks," Thunder said evenly. "We don't steal from anyone. We've never even seen those . . ." His voice fell away; what should he call them? "Those out-laws who slaughtered your friends"? Or "Those brave people who tried to protect their own land"? Sorrow for his country settled in Thunder's throat like a rock. He blurted, "Your soldiers came here with evil intent. Those Tibetans didn't kill them; the soldiers' bad karma willed their own deaths."

This time the long silence was heavy like lead.

The colonel rubbed the back of his neck. "If . . . know them . . . would tell?" he asked clumsily. Then, brushing his hand through the air as if to dismiss any answer they might give, he turned to the translator and added a few foreign words.

"Get out of our sight," the translator snarled, anger blazing in his eyes. "Those poor dead blokes out there were our friends." When the three boys just went on gawking at him, he clapped his hands as if to shoo dogs. "Get out!"

But none of the boys moved. "Is . . . something more?" the colonel asked.

Thunder sucked in a deep breath and let it out.

"Why did you come to our country?"

The colonel gazed at Thunder, waiting for him to say more.

"Do you know our prophecy that when wheels come to Tibet, our country will be ruined?" Thunder asked. "You bring wagons—"

"Do you see any wagons here?" the translator demanded.

But Thunder spoke only to the colonel: "If not now, then later. We both know it's so. And wagons have wheels." There was a pause, tense and terrible. Thunder spread his hands open and looked down at them. "Once I was naive," he said. "I was warned that you fringies came to make maps of our land. But I believed that if fringies had friendly faces, they could not mean us harm." He closed his hands and dropped them to his sides. "But even when you smile at our faces, behind our backs you're making maps. And now I know what maps mean."

"One thing you don't know," the colonel said through his translator, "is that we are under orders to be here. It was not my decision to come to Tibet. I was commanded to come."

"You could have said no."

The colonel shook his head. "You can't guess the consequences that saying no would have meant for me."

"You could have accepted the consequences," Thunder said, "whatever they were." But even as he said it, he realized the hypocrisy of his own words: He, too, could have stayed at Tharpa Dok and accepted the consequences of his own actions. Or he could stop running now, stop running from his responsibility to Pounder, stop running from life at the gompa in all its drudgery, splendor, opportunities, challenges, and even consequences.

He turned toward the door. "Command your soldiers to let us through," he said with quiet dignity.

The colonel crossed the room to Thunder. He held something out in his closed hand, and Thunder saw that it was his own gul-gyan. "No one under my command will bother you again." He dropped the necklace into Thunder's hand. "You have my word." He swept open the door, and Thunder led his friends past one after another of the silent foreign soldiers.

23

▼　▼　▼

THAT NIGHT THEY slept outside, huddled together for warmth. Thunder was drained, yet as if his mind were an enemy sworn to thwart him, he couldn't sleep. Above him the clouded and moonless night spread out less like sky than murky water, bottomless and chill. Below him, every twig, every pebble felt as if Pounder himself were pinching and torturing him.

Beside him, "Dzo!" Seventh Hand whispered, elbowing him gently. "Can't you be still?"

"I'm too worried to sleep. Seventh Hand, if I go back to the gompa . . ." Still blinking up at the sky, he let his voice trail away and waited for Seventh Hand to ask in a shocked tone, "If?" But Seventh Hand was silent, and after a pause Thunder went on. "If I go back, I'll have to do something . . . hard." Again Seventh Hand answered only with silence, and Thunder asked, "Are you awake?"

"I'm awake. I'm listening."

"It's something hard about Pounder."

Instead of asking what Thunder would have to do, Seventh Hand murmured as if from down a long tunnel, "Hard things *do* come along."

It leaped into Thunder's mind that that first night in the kitchen, Seventh Hand had said that all his brothers were at Tharpa Dok. He asked abruptly, "Seventh Hand, is Tharpa Dok your whole— Do you have a home? An ama? An apa?"

The silence stretched out before Seventh Hand said quietly, "No," then added in a more everyday tone, "Will you do the hard thing?"

But Thunder didn't answer. He put his hands under his head to prop it up off the cold ground, then squinted to seek even one star hiding behind the wispy clouds.

In the morning no one said anything more about adventuring. Without any agreement to do so, they began their weary hike home. When they finally neared Tharpa Dok, Thunder hardly noticed the pilgrims who put their tongues out to him as a sign of respect. Respect meant nothing to him; he didn't deserve it.

They walked three abreast through the main gates of Tharpa Dok. With Samjam between them, Thunder and Seventh Hand stood waiting, guilty and ready for punishment. Within seconds older monks noticed them and came running and tore Samjam away. But for the moment there were no questions. Neither what happened nor why concerned anyone—only that Samjam was here and was healthy and whole. Shouts went up: "Our tulku has returned! Sound the conch. Rimpoche! Our tulku! Lord Buddha, our tulku!" Samjam, carried off in a lama's arms, laid his head on the man's shoulder and gazed back at Thunder and Seventh Hand with bleak eyes.

It was only another moment before Seventh Hand was jerked away from Thunder, too. One of the dub dubs dragged him off, slapping at Seventh Hand's head as Lama Thangspa appeared running, his arms out.

Thunder felt a grip on his own arm and turned. It was Zang-po. "Leave me alone," Thunder said, pulling away.

To his surprise, Zang-po opened his mouth as if he would speak, then only dropped Thunder's arm and turned away.

Without the tulku at his side, Thunder drew little attention. He trudged home, his spirit broken and his hopes dashed. His life was so out of control. Not even that hopeless dilemma about his karma mattered to him. Whether he helped Pounder or not, whether he stayed at the gompa or left—none of his problems seemed fixable anymore.

Thunder sat alone before the altar, feeling a load of bricks on his shoulders as he waited for First Aku, yet utterly blank about what to say once he appeared.

"Where is he?" he grudgingly asked Zang-po when the younger boy came in.

"That's what I was going to tell you," Zang-po said, and his voice was strangely absent of animosity. "He's gone up into one of those hermit caves on the cliff to pray for your safety and return."

"My safety and return—he knew I might not return?" Thunder asked, starting to chew on his thumbnail.

Before answering, Zang-po gazed at him steadily. "You didn't treat him right."

Thunder covered his surprise with a snort. "That's a joke, coming from you." But he knew Zang-po spoke the truth.

Zang-po looked away uncomfortably. "Maybe so," he admitted. "But I've never scared him the way you did. Besides," he added wistfully, "I'm not his nephew."

"Go away, Zang-po," Thunder grumbled, as humiliated as if he'd been caught stealing. When he looked up, the boy was gone.

In front of the altar Thunder curled up into the smallest ball possible and dropped into a nightmarish sleep.

When at last he awoke, it was to look up into the face of First Aku, appearing absolutely relieved. "Aku," Thunder stammered, struggling to sit up, "I'm sorry."

First Aku held up his long hand. "Explain nothing."

Thunder shook his head in bewilderment. "Don't you want to know—"

"I tell you, the ordeal is over."

Thunder couldn't meet his uncle's gaze. *"That* one is. But . . ." He looked up, feeling like a condemned man pleading for his life. "Aku, about Pounder. I'm still so afraid."

First Aku nodded. He said gently, "I know."

"You say he's changed—"

"Well, paralyzed." First Aku smiled wryly. "He isn't a butterfly yet."

Thunder looked down. "Nothing you say makes me stop feeling afraid."

"I know."

"But I do trust you." His heart drummed; his tongue felt clumsy and huge, and he couldn't believe he was saying it at last: "If you're advising me to help him, I will."

First Aku's eyes fluttered closed, and his lips moved slightly. Then he leaned way down to where Thunder sat on the floor and lightly placed his open hand over his nephew's heart. "The way Pounder once was, what he has become . . . all is impermanence. Only the heart remains. Yours. Mine. Even his."

Thunder stared down at his uncle's hand on his chest. Under the pressure of his fingers, Thunder could feel the gul-gyan he'd stolen curled up near his heart, too. Then he looked back up at First Aku's relieved face, reached into the pocket of his robe, and took out the gul-gyan. He handed it to his uncle, then buried his face in his hands. "I'm sorry," he moaned.

First Aku stood in stunned silence, dangling the necklace from one finger. In the oven under the khang, the embers glowed, coloring the half-light and First Aku's face. He came down from his full height and, holding the gul-gyan stretched over both open hands, sat on the floor next to his nephew.

Thunder's throat was dry and his voice unsteady. "Zang-po showed me your gul-gyan and"—he could hardly force out the words—"I stole one."

There was such a long silence that Thunder thought First Aku wasn't going to answer. But at last he said, "This gul-gyan is also an indictment of me." Thunder looked up, and from behind his hands he saw that First Aku was turning his single gold ring around and around on his finger. "Nephew," he murmured, "there are so many things you do not understand."

Thunder remembered the soldiers and the expression on the colonel's face. "Once," he said. "But not now."

First Aku moved his eyebrows quizzically but didn't ask questions. Instead he murmured, "I remember running along the paths of Tharpa Dok when I was young, just as you do now." His glance, resting on Thunder, seemed to flicker with the hint of a smile. "Then I imagine my future, when I will inch along only with the help of a stick. For hundreds of years before I arrived at Tharpa Dok, monks have lived their lives here exactly as I have lived mine. They started by dashing around on all the usual important missions of little boys. At the end of their days they were still here, but their aching backs were bent over their walking sticks."

He ran the necklace through his fingers, gazing at it as if it were the ghost of himself at fourteen. "Things are changing. Tibet will change. The ancient prophecy, and now Dondrub's, are so similar. But Dondrub's contains an immediacy—I've told you I fear for Tharpa Dok, for all the gompas. If we were ever attacked—"

"The gompas attacked! But who . . ." Thunder let his voice fall away.

First Aku was staring down at his hands, stroking the gul-gyan. "If that ever happens, then the monks will have to flee. They will fight, perhaps, first. But if they do fight, they will lose. And then they will run." He lifted and dropped his hand with a helpless shake of his head. "It will be easier for some to run than for others."

Thunder thought about all the monks he knew. "You mean . . . Samjam?"

First Aku nodded. "Any tulku would make a precious hostage."

"So are you suggesting that Samjam could use these gul-gyan to buy his way out of trouble?" Thunder remembered trying to pay off the soldier with his uncle's gul-gyan. "Aku, it might not work."

First Aku's eyes widened as if it were jarring that Thunder understood his idea so quickly. "But, Nephew, it might work. Rarely can one do more than try."

"Who would ever attack a holy place like this?"

First Aku didn't answer the question. Instead he held up the necklace and said, "This gul-gyan—all these gul-gyan—are for Samjam. A sort of insurance. For a long time during his last incarnation, I worried about his future. Yet I did nothing. Then Samjam went beyond sorrow under suspicious circumstances. He was only seventeen, and I was bitter. I began to collect—I don't know, perhaps steal—these gul-gyan for him in his next incarnation. They are not perfect insurance, but they are the best I can provide for him."

"You didn't steal them. Not really."

First Aku shrugged a tight and dubious shrug. "Opinions might differ on that question," he said with a wry smile. "But Lama Tsab-Chang and I have always had different philosophies about how to protect the tulku of Tharpa Dok. If we did not, then these would officially be set aside for Samjam's safety. Anyway, that is what I tell myself. Perhaps I make excuses. If I had been told by a fortune-teller when I was twenty that one day I would steal Tharpa Dok's gul-gyan for my own purposes, I would have laughed."

"Not for your purposes. You kept them for Samjam, and only because you care."

"Sometimes the compassionate and the criminal wear the same chuba. Now the time has come for me to put absolute trust in Lord Buddha and to leave such scheming to the young." He motioned for Thunder to hold out his hand, then spilled the necklace into it.

"Don't give me your gul-gyan," Thunder said, shaking

his head as his uncle started toward where the rest of his necklaces were hidden.

"Yes. My chest feels cut open from the things I have admitted out loud. I must give you my gul-gyan, and I must give them now. Most must be for Samjam. But some are for you." He reached for the brick behind which the necklaces lay. "They will be a memento of one special day in your life when"—he threw back his head and laughed—"when you drove crazy a whole gompa of wise old holy men with a caper that resolved itself in the end. And remember," he added seriously, "a prank as mischievous as filching a tulku . . ." He smiled. "Never tell."

"No, Aku," Thunder said with his first weary smile of the day. "If not to you, then to no one."

First Aku extracted the gul-gyan and put the heavy box in Thunder's hands.

As before, Thunder shook his head. "Don't. I would only give mine away."

First Aku's eyebrows rose. "To?"

Thunder shrugged. "Maybe to Seventh Hand."

"The kitchen boy?"

"Yes. I couldn't bear . . ." Thunder began, then said simply, "He has never had anything of his own."

First Aku gazed at Thunder appraisingly. "Well, then. Perhaps you should."

"Should?" Thunder asked, glancing up.

"Should give them to him."

Thunder opened the box lid and in silence looked

down at the beads. Silver and coral and turquoise and gold, some rough, some smooth, some carved with tiny letters or even scenes. "Or Dolma," he said as the possibility dawned on him.

"Ah, yes. I would like that, too. Anyone else?"

Thunder was quiet for a long time before he said unwillingly, "Maybe one to Zang-po. But only because of something he once said." Then he blurted, "Aku, do you realize that you . . . you favor me over Zang-po?"

"Do I?" Gyalo asked, looking up sharply. He reached out and squeezed Thunder's shoulder. "You are my teacher," he said. He unhooked the brass water bottle that hung at his waist, took a sip of water, and touched the corners of his lips with his finger. When he looked at Thunder again, his eyes were shrewd. "But there will be many more Seventh Hands in your life. And Dolmas."

"Not Zang-pos, I hope," Thunder grumbled.

But First Aku flashed a flat smile. "Many, *many* more Zang-pos. Soon you will have given away every gul-gyan. Don't forget, you must keep all but a few for the tulku."

"But Aku, once mine are gone, what will I give?"

First Aku regarded him pensively. "Ah."

24

▼ ▼ ▼

THUNDER GLANCED AT the door. "Did you hear someone?"

"Ulay! Ulay!" a man cried, and the door began opening, creaking as it swung back on its leather hinges.

"Brother!" "Apa!" First Aku and Thunder cried simultaneously. Thunder couldn't believe that after all this time there stood his father, silhouetted in the doorway with his horse behind him.

Thunder scrambled to his feet, overjoyed, and ran to press his forehead against his father's in greeting. For so many months he had waited here where he didn't belong, bargaining with Lord Buddha and counting the days. He was certain why Apa was here; it was as if Apa had already invited him home.

But something in his father's posture and the expression on his face paralyzed Thunder. From behind him First Aku asked quietly, "Brother, what has put this new melancholy into your eyes?"

Thunder turned to look at First Aku, wondering what he was perceiving so clearly about Apa that Thunder sensed but couldn't quite put his finger on.

Apa sank down, exhausted, on the khang. His hands were tight fists where he gripped the edge of the khang, as if his knucklebones might break through the skin. "Only we two are left, Brother," he finally murmured without looking up. "Tendruk is gone."

"Gone?" Gyalo gasped.

Apa nodded. But though he opened and closed his mouth, he seemed unable to explain.

"Gone? You mean? But how?" Aku strode across the room, folded up his long body, and sat on the floor at his brother's feet.

Apa cleared his throat. "Avalanche." His face was blank, his eyes dismal. "We were riding. I was behind. Tendruk looked back at me. He called something. Then he laughed. And I heard a cracking sound. From above . . . avalanche." He turned his face away and squeezed his eyes shut. "That's all. Avalanche."

Thunder had never seen a grown man cry, and now there were two. He wished he could cry, too. Instead he heard a seemingly distant voice that had to be his own, though he felt no responsibility for its cold words: "Never in my life did Second Aku say a single kind word to me."

"It was that way, was it?" Gyalo asked, looking with sorrow not at Thunder but at his brother, though Rinjing was still turned away. "If only . . ." First Aku continued. But then he shook his head. "Nephew, your spirit is older than my little brother's. You could have taught him so much."

"I older?" Thunder asked in bewilderment. "When I was born, he was already grown. *I* teach *him*?"

With his eyes closed, First Aku put his head all the way back and groaned. "Why do you find it so hard to accept that you have learned something during your life?" he asked the ceiling. Then he leaned forward and laid his forehead against Thunder's cabinet.

But still Thunder felt dull-witted. "Learned? You mean . . ." He looked first at First Aku, still with his head against the cabinet, then at Apa, so thoroughly out of place here as he gawked blankly back and forth between his brother and son. Apa could not understand First Aku's kind of talk any more than if he were speaking Chinese. And something in Thunder's mind clicked: something about himself, about karma, about learning, even about Pounder. The truth could have knocked Thunder to the floor: Whether I meant to or not, I have changed over completely from Apa's world to First Aku's.

In time the men began telling cheerful stories of their brother's life. "I remember," Apa said, gazing off at a vision of his younger life, "how Tendruk loved to wake me when I was sleeping. He would tie a cucumber on a string, then climb up high on a beam, or in a tree if I was sleeping outside, and dangle that cucumber down and tickle my nose with it. Remember that, Gyalo?"

First Aku uttered a clipped laugh: "Yes. And whenever I was discouraged, Tendruk would tell me some heart-wrenching story about how his friend's favorite horse had rolled on him and crushed his leg, or some such. By the end of his tale I would have completely forgotten my own petty crisis. I would be standing there with my mouth hanging open, feeling so sorry for the poor boy."

Apa added, "Then Tendruk would say, 'Aha! Your troubles aren't so bad after all, are they?' and off he'd go."

Looking down so that Thunder couldn't see his eyes, Gyalo began smoothing and smoothing his robe over his knees. "Later he changed," he murmured. He brushed his sleeve across his eyes, then motioned to Thunder. "Will you show your apa to the stables? Help him brush down his horse and bring in his pack."

Standing beside Apa and holding the reins of the horse, Thunder felt unexplainably shy. "Your ama sent you new boots," Apa said, digging into a saddlebag. He handed Thunder splendid and unusual boots, white with exquisite embroidery along the top. Thunder held them in his arms like a baby, and they both looked down at them uncomfortably; clearly they were for a smaller boy. "Tell her I loved them," Thunder said.

Nodding his approval, Apa murmured, "What's the harm?"

"Somebody can use them," Thunder added, grinning as he imagined how Zang-po would prance, wearing them.

When they had settled the horse, Apa faced Thunder and spoke. "I came here . . . Ama and I thought you both should know about your second aku. That was part of it. But also . . ." He smiled shyly and ducked his head. "Thunder, things have changed in Chu Lungba. People's hearts have softened toward you. Your mistakes don't matter so much anymore. Besides that, without Tendruk to help with the farm . . ." Gazing away as he envisioned his home, Apa swept his hand through the air dismissively.

Thunder sensed what was coming. He wished he could stop Apa from asking the important question, but instead the words rushed at him like rocks: "Are you happy here, son?"

Thunder laid his trembling hand on the horse's bony head. "What did you expect me to find here at the gompa?" he asked with the sudden boldness of a shy, cornered child. There was a long silence while Apa searched his son's face. Thunder didn't want to say more. But he knew these were things that he needed to say and that his apa needed to hear. So he took a deep breath. "When you sent me here"—he forced himself to go on—"did you think Tharpa Dok would be a temporary home? A place to hide out? Or did you intend for me to fall in love with this life?"

"Intend?" Apa looked puzzled. "I don't know. You

were so determined to break your back under the plow. It's what I've done all my life. It's what Joker must do, and Razim. Tendruk gave his days to the plow, too. But you," he murmured, "you were always different."

"Me? Different? No! I was the one always doing what I was told, always following along, always being the dumb yak."

"Do you think so . . . truly?" Apa looked hard and long at Thunder. "Dolma was the one," he said, his voice heavy with thought, "who always saw clearly. She knew you. For years she'd been warning me that you weren't right for the farm."

Thunder gaped at him, astonished. "You mean, while you and Ama were busy laying plans for me to work the farm every day of my life, she . . . ?" But he thought, too, of what Dolma's life was like. Like Thunder, she always did what she was told. She served others. Always there would be others she must serve and obey. Would Dolma ever have the good fortune to crash out of her world of *should*s and *must*s to blunder by chance into who she was meant to be? Thunder feared that that chance would never find Dolma.

But it had found him.

His father was nodding. "Dolma was right," he said. "I see it in your face." Gently he brushed his fingertips against Thunder's cheek. "Shall I tell your ama that Dolma was right?"

Thunder gripped his father by both shoulders, touched his forehead to Apa's, and held it there, grateful that Apa hadn't made him say aloud those awful and wonderful words: I need to stay here.

Then it was time for prayer assembly. Apa was going along, too. But Thunder set off first in the other direction. He held his uncommon conch with spirals that turned in a different direction from most, his singular conch that had needed to pass through foreign hands before it came into this particular pair of Tibetan hands, where it belonged.

As he scampered up stone staircases and ramps, it flashed into his mind that when he'd asked First Aku what he could give after the gul-gyan were gone, Aku had only said, "Ah." Not much of an answer, Thunder thought, but knowing First Aku, he would say more in time.

Then, from the highest roof of his gompa, Thunder lifted his conch to his mouth. With his head thrown back and his eyes closed, he launched his call up into the vast Tibetan sky.

AFTERWORD

▼ ▼ ▼

In 1904 Great Britain sent Colonel Francis Younghusband, with three hundred soldiers, to invade Tibet. Hearing that foreign troops were marching on the capital city of Lhasa, the thirteenth Dalai Lama fled from his country.

When the soldiers arrived in Lhasa, the local people along their route clapped their hands wildly. Younghusband and his troops thought that they were cheering. Actually Tibetans at that time clapped their hands to drive away evil spirits. They only wanted the foreigners to leave.

Younghusband forced the Dalai Lama's regent, Lamoshar Lobsang Gyaltsen, to sign a trade treaty with Britain. To the Tibetans' relief, the British soldiers remained in Lhasa for only two months. However, the treaty that Younghusband thrust upon Tibet was the first step in forcing the country to open its borders to foreigners.

In 1949 one hundred thousand troops of the newly established Chinese Communist government easily conquered Tibet. This time the troops did not leave. Chinese soldiers have occupied Tibet since that time.

As the Chinese presence in Tibet strengthened, and Tibetans began to openly resist Chinese rule, China repeatedly violated its treaty, destroying more than six thousand historical buildings, particularly gompas like Tharpa Dok. Today more Chinese than Tibetans live in Tibet, and Tibetan schoolchildren must learn their lessons in Chinese. The Tibetan culture has been largely destroyed.

Those Tibetans still in their homeland fight a daily battle to keep what little is left of their culture. Many Tibetans have emigrated. In 1959 even His Holiness The Fourteenth Dalai Lama fled from the Chinese invaders, just as his predecessor fled from the British.

Since leaving Lhasa more than forty years ago, His Holiness has never been able to return to his homeland.

I became interested in Tibet when I happened across two fascinating books, *Magic and Mystery in Tibet* and *My Journey to Lhasa,* both by French explorer Alexandra David-Neel. The first prominent female explorer and journalist of the twentieth century, she traveled through Asia, mainly from 1911 through 1925. She adopted a young Sikkimese lama, Yongden, as her son, and even became a lama in her own right.

When Tibet was still closed to foreigners, David-Neel sneaked into the country in disguise, much like the foreigner in the beginning of this book. She reached the forbidden city of Lhasa in 1924. During this dangerous journey, David-Neel had several risky encounters with Tibetans, similar to Thunder's confrontation with the foreigner. As I read David-Neel's hair-raising account of being recognized as a foreigner, I wondered what that experience felt like to the Tibetans who met her.

During the two years I lived in Hong Kong, I researched turn-of-the-century Tibet at the University of Hong Kong. I am grateful to the librarians there, who gave me free access to the university's unusual collection of missionaries' and explorers' accounts of life in Tibet around 1900.

In Hong Kong and Taipei, I interviewed emigrated Tibetan monks about day-to-day life in the gompas one hundred years ago. I appreciate the aid of Hugh Thomas, who helped arrange these interviews for me and who kindly translated.

This book evolved out of my deep love and respect for the Tibetan people and their fading civilization. Tragically, since Thunder's day, Padmasambhava's eighth-century prophecy has been fulfilled: Planes fly over Tibet, wheeled vehicles travel its roads, and countless Tibetans have been forced to leave their homeland. They are scattered like ants around the world.

Some of the books I used in my research were

Bell, William. *The People of Tibet.* Oxford: Clarendon Press, 1924.

Carey, William. *Adventures in Tibet.* New York: Baker & Taylor, 1905.

David-Neel, Alexandra. *Magic and Mystery in Tibet.* New York: Claude Kendall, 1932.

————. *My Journey to Lhasa.* New York: Harper & Bros., 1927.

French, Patrick. *Younghusband.* London: HarperCollins, 1994.

Hedin, Sven. *Adventures in Tibet.* London: Hurst & Blackett, 1904.

————. *My Life as an Explorer.* Garden City, New York: Garden City Publishing Co., 1925.

Hopkirk, Peter. *Trespassers on the Roof of the World.* London: John Murray, 1982.

Huc, Evariste Regis. *Recollections of a Journey through Tartary, Thibet and China.* London: Longman, 1846.

Macdonald, David. *The Land of the Lama.* London: Seeley, Service, 1929.

Rijnhard, Susie. *With the Tibetans in Tent and Temple.* Chicago: Revell, 1909.

Rockhill, William Woodville. *Land of the Lamas.* New York: Century, 1891.

Ronaldshay, Lawrence. *Lands of the Thunderbolt.* London: Constable, 1923.

Waddell, L. Austine. *The Buddhism of Tibet.* London: W. H. Allen, 1895.

———. *Lhasa and Its Mysteries.* London: John Murray, 1905.

GLOSSARY

▼ ▼ ▼

Aku	Uncle.
Ama	Mother.
Apa	Father.
Buddha	Siddhartha Gautama, the founder of Buddhism. *Buddha* means "enlightened one."
Butter lamp	A socketed bowl filled with butter and having a wick in the center.
Chokang	A chapel in a private home.
Chuba	A Tibetan layman's main garment. It is a belted, knee-length tunic with sleeves that come down over the hands.
Chura	Cheese dried until it is hard.
Dalai Lama	Supreme political and religious leader of traditional Tibet.
Dibshing	A sliver of wood believed hidden in the nests of crows. Traditional Tibetans believed that it could make a person invisible.
Dub dub	A monastery soldier.
Dzo	Animal that is half yak, half cow.

Fringie	Caucasian foreigner.
Go beyond sorrow	To die.
Gompa	A Tibetan monastery.
Go slowly	Good-bye to someone leaving.
Gul-gyan	Valuable necklaces, used to pay funeral expenses at their owner's death.
Ingi-li	English.
Karma	Buddhist law of moral compensation— i.e., for every action there is a reaction.
Khamstan	A monastery dormitory, each one used by monks from a particular geographical area of Tibet.
Khang	A stone platform heated by an oven underneath. Used for sleeping at night or sitting during the day.
Khata	"Scarf of happiness." Presented to a person on ceremonial visits, when asking a favor, wishing someone good luck, or as a thank-you.
Kushog	Sir.
Lama	A high-ranking Tibetan monk.
Lhasa	The capital city of Tibet.
Mani stones	Celebrated groups of stones carved with mantras, which usually mark important sites.
Mantra	Chanted words, spoken in Sanskrit, used in rituals to concentrate one's attention.
Mastiff	Large Tibetan dog with lionlike head.

Momo	Sweet pastry.
Nirvana	Buddhist heaven.
Ocean of Wisdom	The Dalai Lama.
Prayer cylinder/ prayer wheel	Copper or silver cylinder, usually small and on a handle, that contains rolls of paper inscribed with mantras. To pray, one swings the cylinder around.
Prayer flags	Bits of cloth that are considered luck talismans. They are stamped with prayers or images of gods and are tied to ropes, trees, bridges, rifles, etc.
Rimpoche	A polite address for a lama, meaning "precious one."
Torma	Conical cakes of tsampa, used in various ceremonies.
Tsampa	Flour made from roasted barley and eaten as a staple food in Tibet.
Tulku	A high-ranking lama who is the reincarnation of a saintly person or the incarnation of a nonhuman entity.
Ulay	Hello.
Wheel of life	Circular depiction of the six areas of rebirth, usually shown held in the claws of a monster.
Yak	Tibetan beast of burden, similar to the bison.

About the Author

Born in Rochester, New York, **CHERYL AYLWARD WHITESEL** has also lived in Illinois, Louisiana, and Michigan and spent twelve years in Asia. After her son was born, she abandoned her law career and decided to pursue the dream she had since the age of eight—to write books for young people. She and her husband, Paul Cassingham, have a fifteen-year-old son, Ross, and a talking parakeet named Ping. Ms. Whitesel lives in Western Springs, Illinois. This is her first book.